ALEX ALICE

CASTLE
IN
THE
STARS

THE SPACE RACE OF 1869

First Second
New York

First Second

English translation by Anne and Owen Smith
English translation © 2017 by Roaring Brook Press,
a division of Holtzbrinck Publishing Holdings Limited Partnership

Published by First Second
First Second is an imprint of Roaring Brook Press,
a division of Holtzbrinck Publishing Holdings Limited Partnership
175 Fifth Avenue, New York, New York 10010
All rights reserved

Library of Congress Control Number: 2016961590

ISBN: 978-1-62672-493-8

Our books may be purchased in bulk for promotional, educational, or business use.
Please contact your local bookseller or the Macmillan Corporate and Premium Sales Department
at (800) 221-7945 ext. 5442 or by e-mail at MacmillanSpecialMarkets@macmillan.com.

Originally published in 2014 in French by Rue de Sèvres as *Le château des étoiles - 1869: La conquête de l'espace - Volume I*
French text and illustrations by Alex Alice © 2014 Rue de Sèvres, Paris.
First American edition 2017
Book design by Chris Dickey

Printed in China by RR Donnelley Asia Printing Solutions Ltd., Dongguan City, Guangdong Province
10 9 8 7 6 5 4 3 2 1

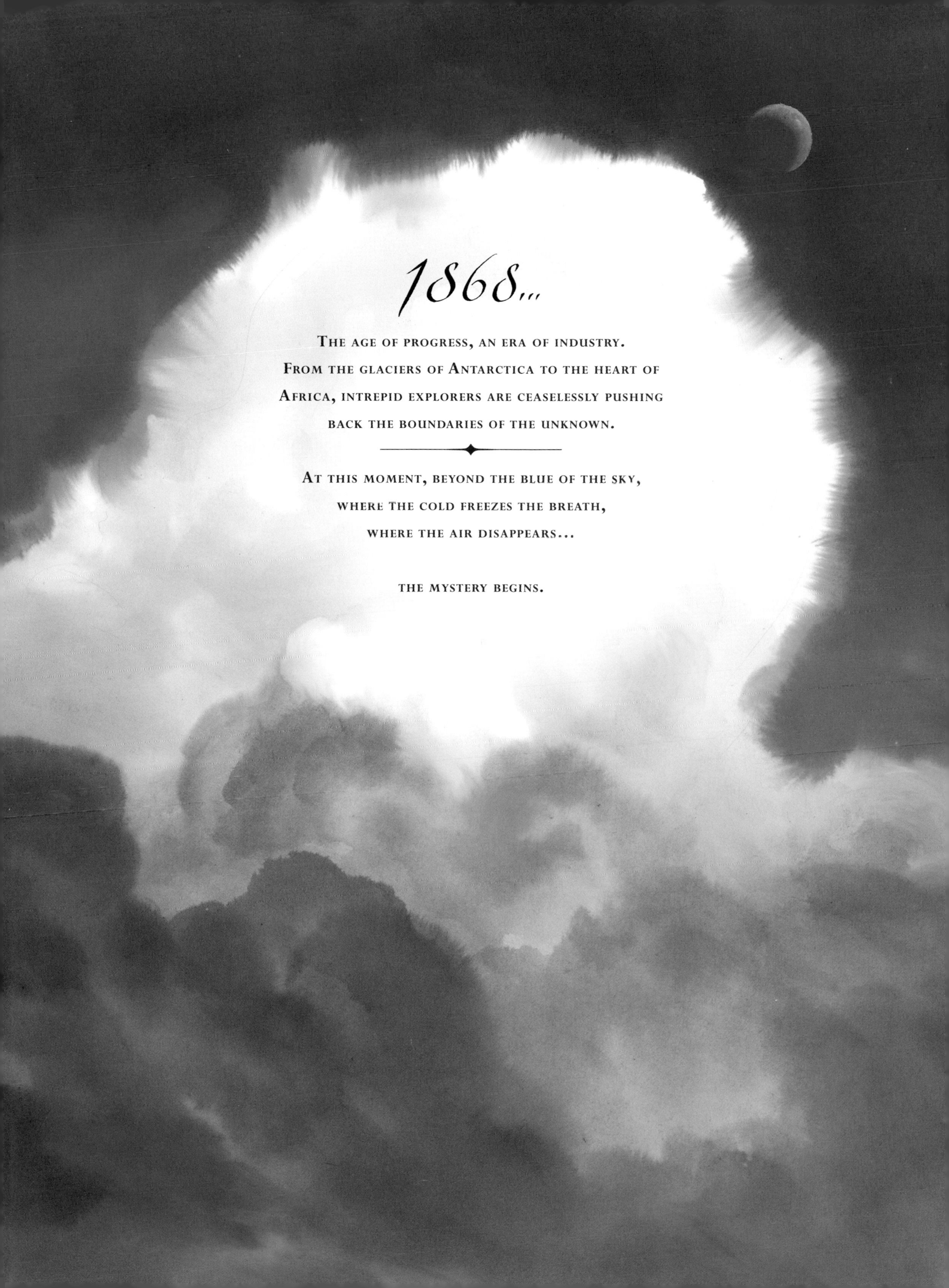

1868...

THE AGE OF PROGRESS, AN ERA OF INDUSTRY.
FROM THE GLACIERS OF ANTARCTICA TO THE HEART OF
AFRICA, INTREPID EXPLORERS ARE CEASELESSLY PUSHING
BACK THE BOUNDARIES OF THE UNKNOWN.

AT THIS MOMENT, BEYOND THE BLUE OF THE SKY,
WHERE THE COLD FREEZES THE BREATH,
WHERE THE AIR DISAPPEARS...

THE MYSTERY BEGINS.

CHAPTER 1

THE SECRET OF AETHER

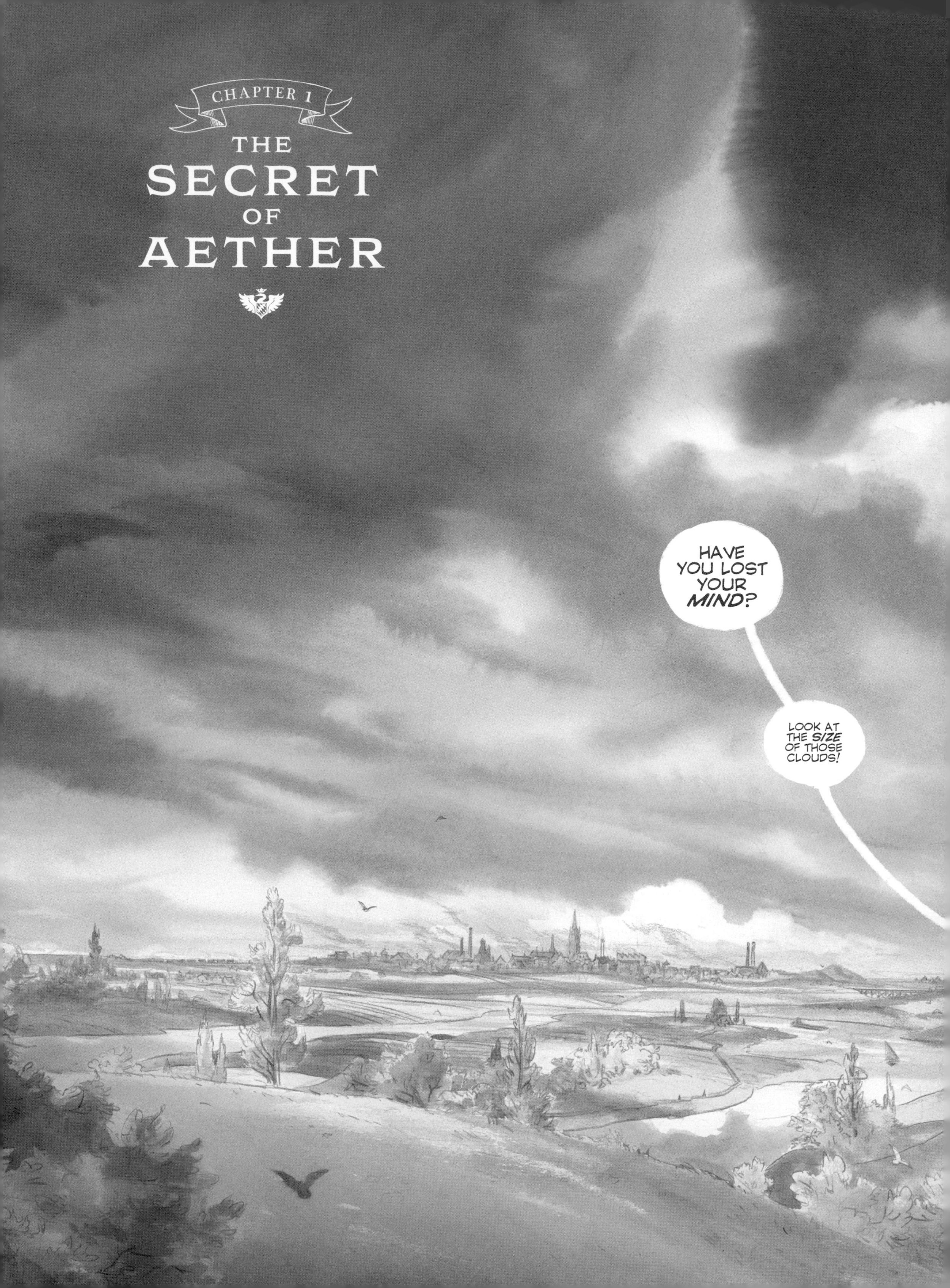
HAVE YOU LOST YOUR *MIND*?
LOOK AT THE *SIZE* OF THOSE CLOUDS!

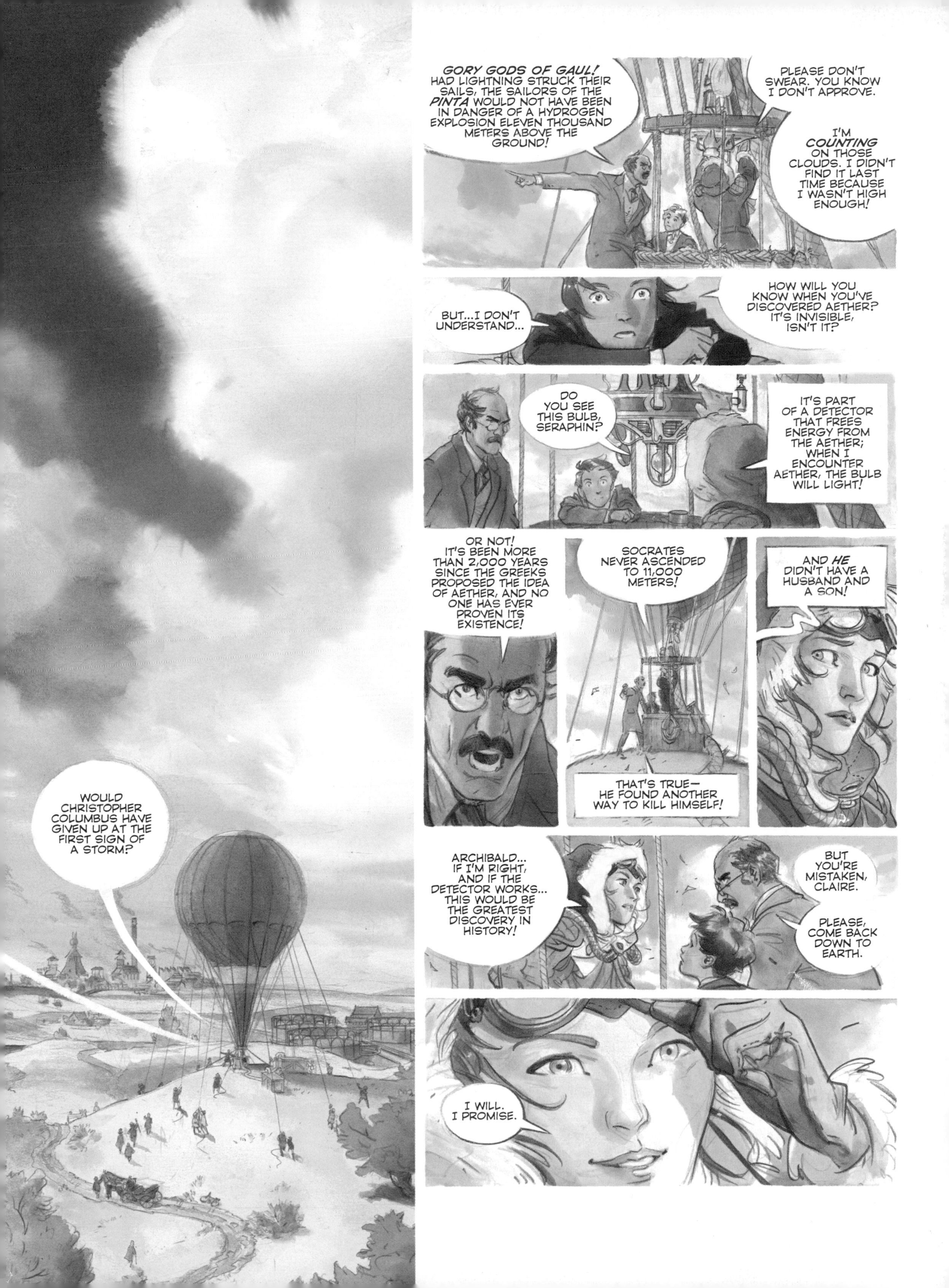
WOULD CHRISTOPHER COLUMBUS HAVE GIVEN UP AT THE FIRST SIGN OF A STORM?
GORY GODS OF GAUL! HAD LIGHTNING STRUCK THEIR SAILS, THE SAILORS OF THE PINTA WOULD NOT HAVE BEEN IN DANGER OF A HYDROGEN EXPLOSION ELEVEN THOUSAND METERS ABOVE THE GROUND!
PLEASE DON'T SWEAR. YOU KNOW I DON'T APPROVE.
I'M COUNTING ON THOSE CLOUDS. I DIDN'T FIND IT LAST TIME BECAUSE I WASN'T HIGH ENOUGH!
BUT...I DON'T UNDERSTAND...
HOW WILL YOU KNOW WHEN YOU'VE DISCOVERED AETHER? IT'S INVISIBLE, ISN'T IT?
DO YOU SEE THIS BULB, SERAPHIN?
IT'S PART OF A DETECTOR THAT FREES ENERGY FROM THE AETHER; WHEN I ENCOUNTER AETHER, THE BULB WILL LIGHT!
OR NOT! IT'S BEEN MORE THAN 2,000 YEARS SINCE THE GREEKS PROPOSED THE IDEA OF AETHER, AND NO ONE HAS EVER PROVEN ITS EXISTENCE!
SOCRATES NEVER ASCENDED TO 11,000 METERS!
THAT'S TRUE— HE FOUND ANOTHER WAY TO KILL HIMSELF!
AND HE DIDN'T HAVE A HUSBAND AND A SON!
ARCHIBALD... IF I'M RIGHT, AND IF THE DETECTOR WORKS... THIS WOULD BE THE GREATEST DISCOVERY IN HISTORY!
BUT YOU'RE MISTAKEN, CLAIRE.
PLEASE, COME BACK DOWN TO EARTH.
I WILL. I PROMISE.

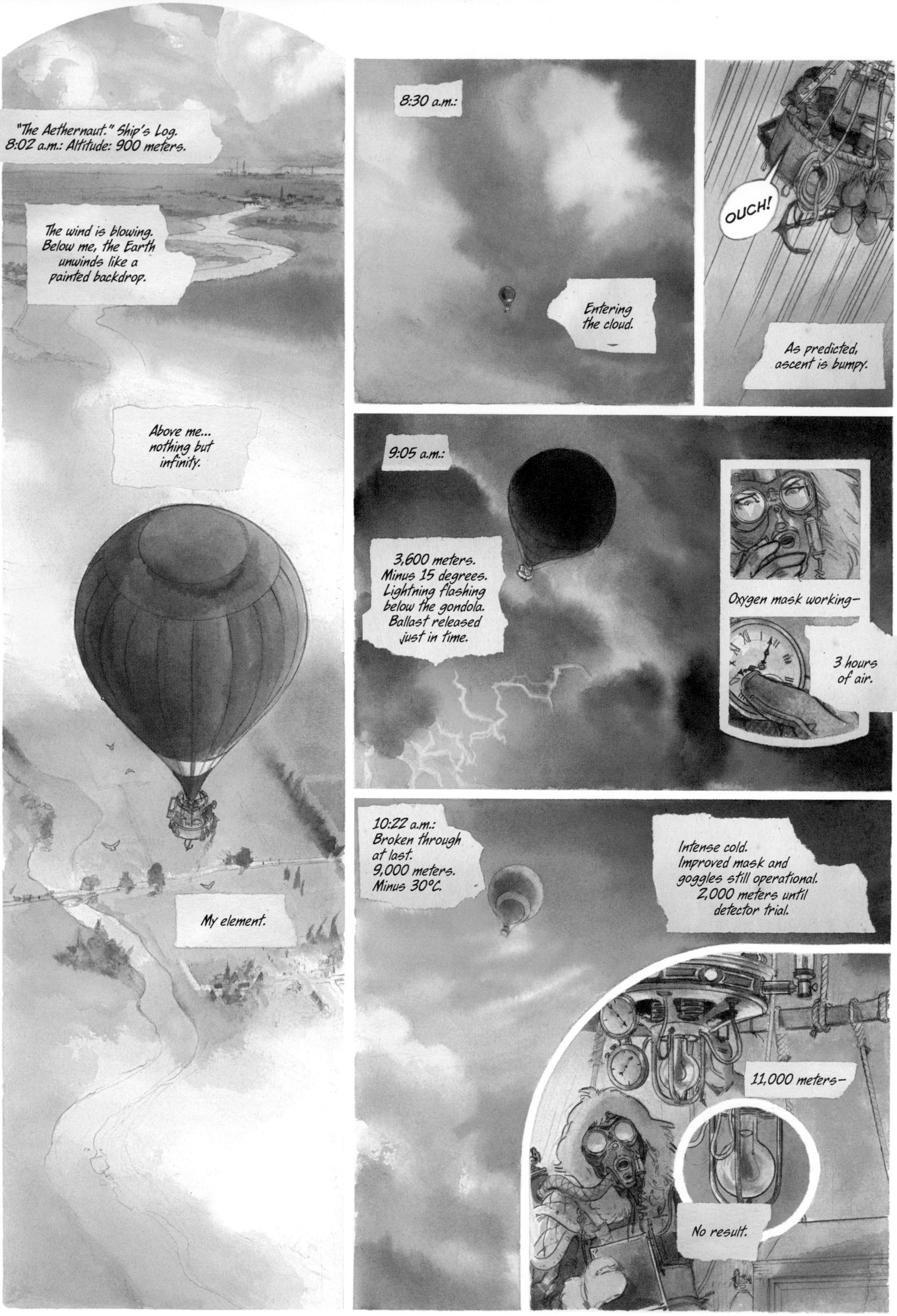
"The Aethernaut." Ship's Log.
8:02 a.m.: Altitude: 900 meters.
The wind is blowing. Below me, the Earth unwinds like a painted backdrop.
Above me... nothing but infinity.
My element.
8:30 a.m.:
Entering the cloud.
OUCH!
As predicted, ascent is bumpy.
9:05 a.m.:
3,600 meters. Minus 15 degrees. Lightning flashing below the gondola. Ballast released just in time.
Oxygen mask working—
3 hours of air.
10:22 a.m.: Broken through at last. 9,000 meters. Minus 30°C.
Intense cold. Improved mask and goggles still operational. 2,000 meters until detector trial.
11,000 meters—
No result.

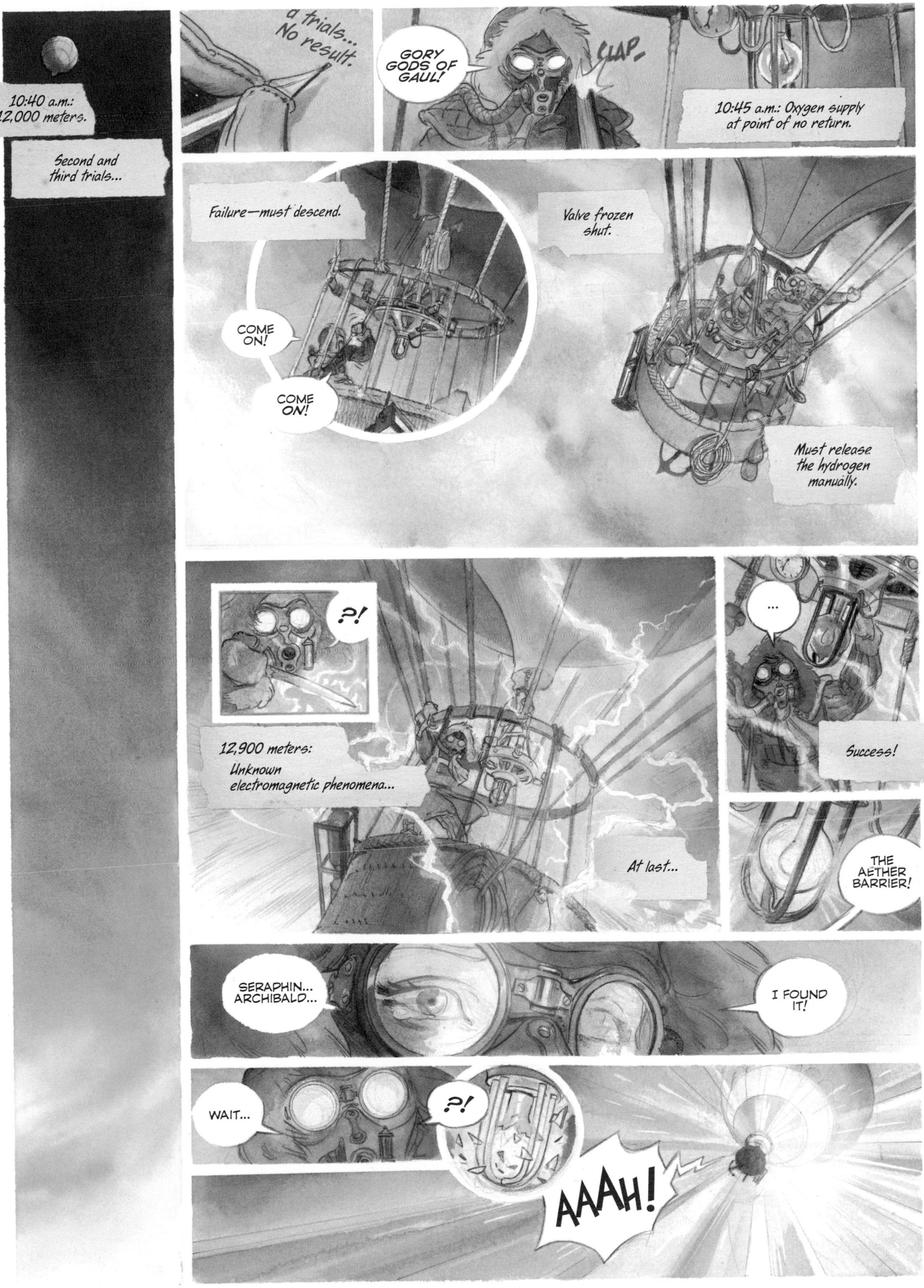
10:40 a.m.: 12,000 meters.
Second and third trials...
a trials... No result.
GORY GODS OF GAUL!
CLAP_
10:45 a.m.: Oxygen supply at point of no return.
Failure—must descend.
COME ON!
COME ON!
Valve frozen shut.
Must release the hydrogen manually.
?!
12,900 meters: Unknown electromagnetic phenomena...
At last...
...
Success!
THE AETHER BARRIER!
SERAPHIN... ARCHIBALD...
I FOUND IT!
WAIT...
?!
AAAH!

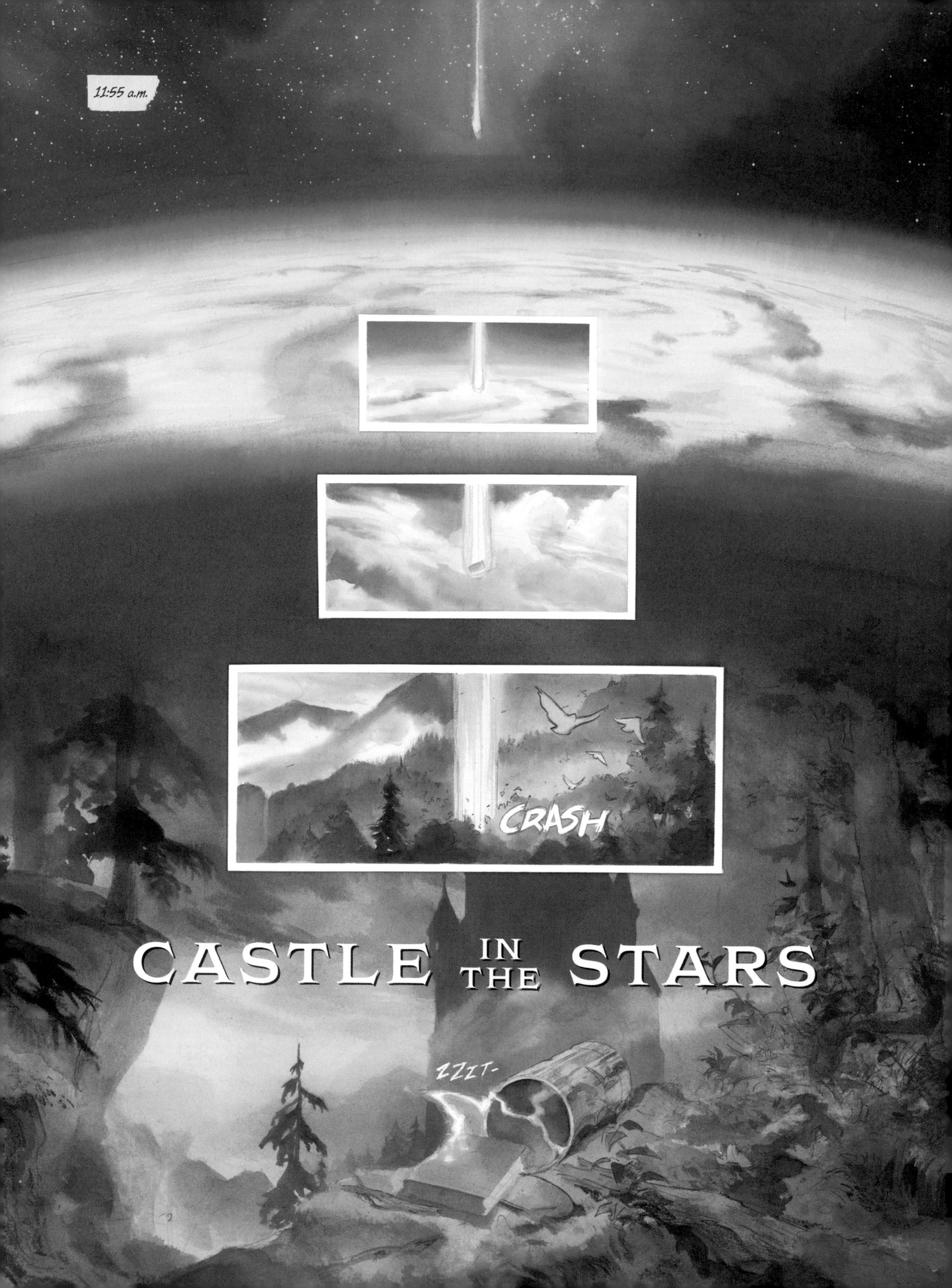
11:55 a.m.
CRASH
CASTLE IN THE STARS
ZZZT-

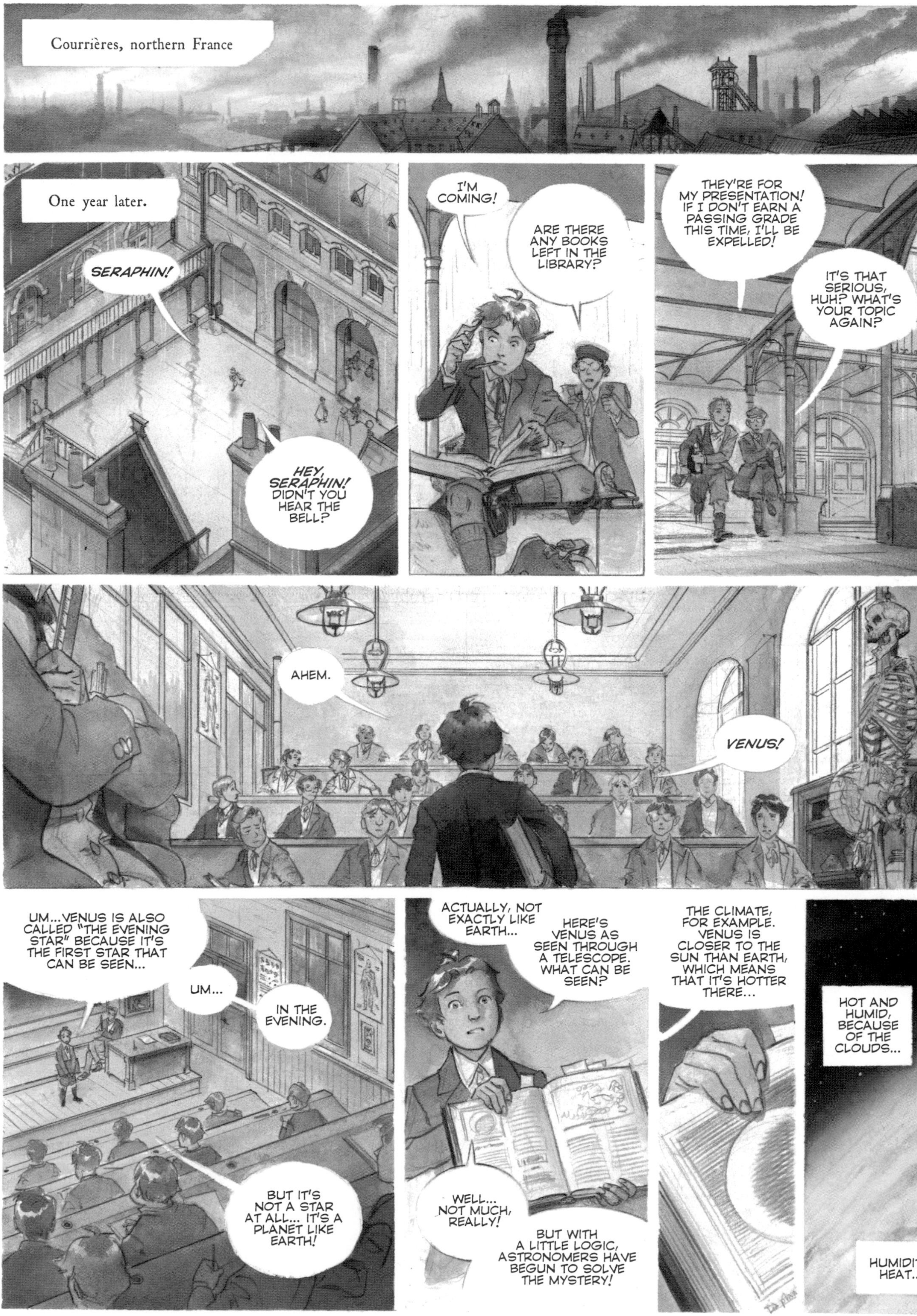

Courrières, northern France
One year later.
SERAPHIN!
HEY, SERAPHIN! DIDN'T YOU HEAR THE BELL?
I'M COMING!
ARE THERE ANY BOOKS LEFT IN THE LIBRARY?
THEY'RE FOR MY PRESENTATION! IF I DON'T EARN A PASSING GRADE THIS TIME, I'LL BE EXPELLED!
IT'S THAT SERIOUS, HUH? WHAT'S YOUR TOPIC AGAIN?
AHEM.
VENUS!
UM...VENUS IS ALSO CALLED "THE EVENING STAR" BECAUSE IT'S THE FIRST STAR THAT CAN BE SEEN...
UM...
IN THE EVENING.
BUT IT'S NOT A STAR AT ALL... IT'S A PLANET LIKE EARTH!
ACTUALLY, NOT EXACTLY LIKE EARTH...
HERE'S VENUS AS SEEN THROUGH A TELESCOPE. WHAT CAN BE SEEN?
WELL... NOT MUCH, REALLY!
BUT WITH A LITTLE LOGIC, ASTRONOMERS HAVE BEGUN TO SOLVE THE MYSTERY!
THE CLIMATE, FOR EXAMPLE. VENUS IS CLOSER TO THE SUN THAN EARTH, WHICH MEANS THAT IT'S HOTTER THERE...
HOT AND HUMID, BECAUSE OF THE CLOUDS...
HUMIDITY, HEAT...

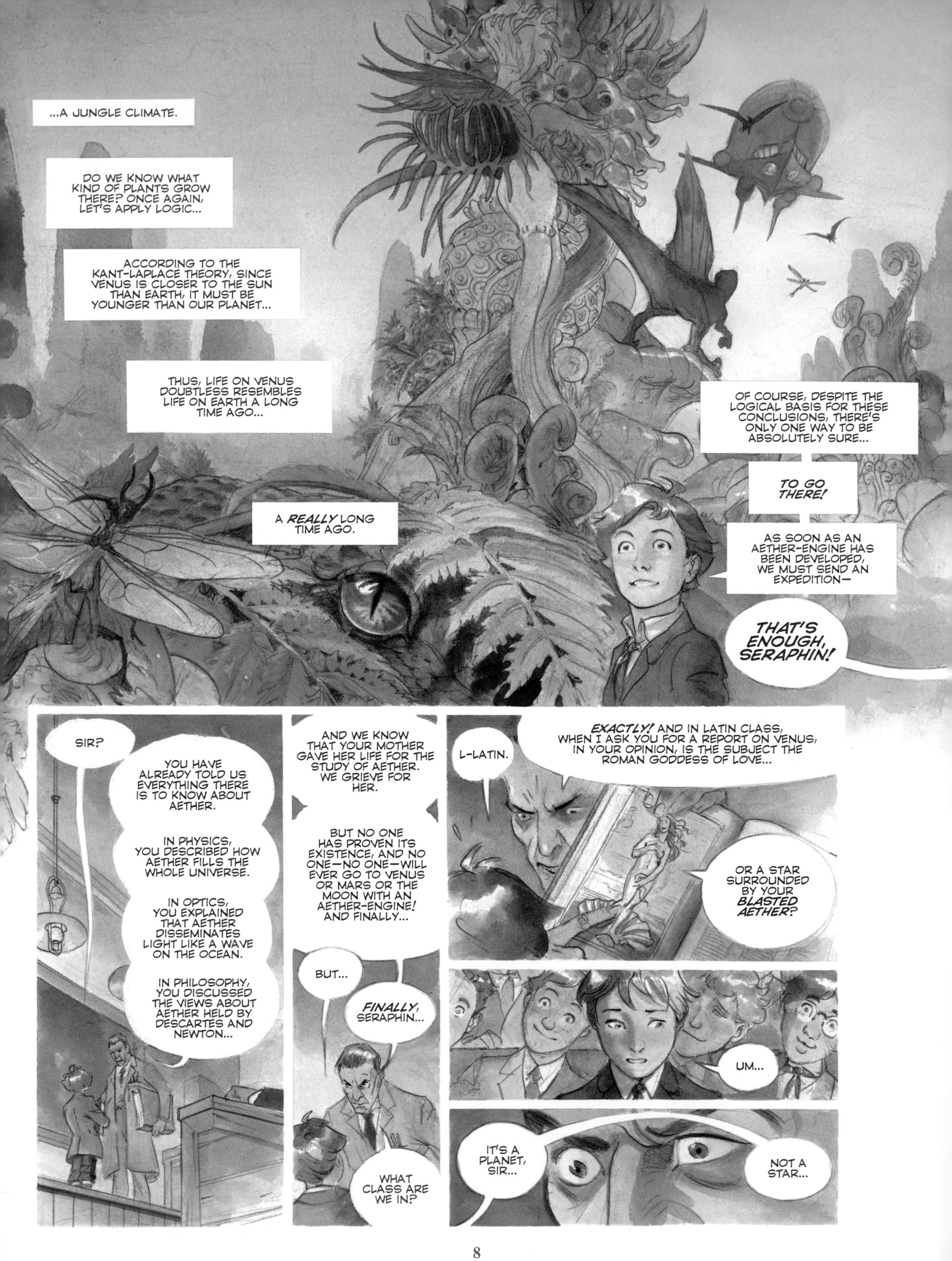
...A JUNGLE CLIMATE.
DO WE KNOW WHAT KIND OF PLANTS GROW THERE? ONCE AGAIN, LET'S APPLY LOGIC...
ACCORDING TO THE KANT-LAPLACE THEORY, SINCE VENUS IS CLOSER TO THE SUN THAN EARTH, IT MUST BE YOUNGER THAN OUR PLANET...
THUS, LIFE ON VENUS DOUBTLESS RESEMBLES LIFE ON EARTH A LONG TIME AGO...
A *REALLY* LONG TIME AGO.
OF COURSE, DESPITE THE LOGICAL BASIS FOR THESE CONCLUSIONS, THERE'S ONLY ONE WAY TO BE ABSOLUTELY SURE...
TO GO THERE!
AS SOON AS AN AETHER-ENGINE HAS BEEN DEVELOPED, WE MUST SEND AN EXPEDITION—
THAT'S ENOUGH, SERAPHIN!
SIR?
YOU HAVE ALREADY TOLD US EVERYTHING THERE IS TO KNOW ABOUT AETHER.
IN PHYSICS, YOU DESCRIBED HOW AETHER FILLS THE WHOLE UNIVERSE.
IN OPTICS, YOU EXPLAINED THAT AETHER DISSEMINATES LIGHT LIKE A WAVE ON THE OCEAN.
IN PHILOSOPHY, YOU DISCUSSED THE VIEWS ABOUT AETHER HELD BY DESCARTES AND NEWTON...
AND WE KNOW THAT YOUR MOTHER GAVE HER LIFE FOR THE STUDY OF AETHER. WE GRIEVE FOR HER.
BUT NO ONE HAS PROVEN ITS EXISTENCE, AND NO ONE—NO ONE—WILL EVER GO TO VENUS OR MARS OR THE MOON WITH AN AETHER-ENGINE! AND FINALLY...
BUT...
FINALLY, SERAPHIN...
WHAT CLASS ARE WE IN?
L-LATIN.
EXACTLY! AND IN LATIN CLASS, WHEN I ASK YOU FOR A REPORT ON VENUS, IN YOUR OPINION, IS THE SUBJECT THE ROMAN GODDESS OF LOVE...
OR A STAR SURROUNDED BY YOUR *BLASTED AETHER*?
UM...
IT'S A PLANET, SIR...
NOT A STAR...

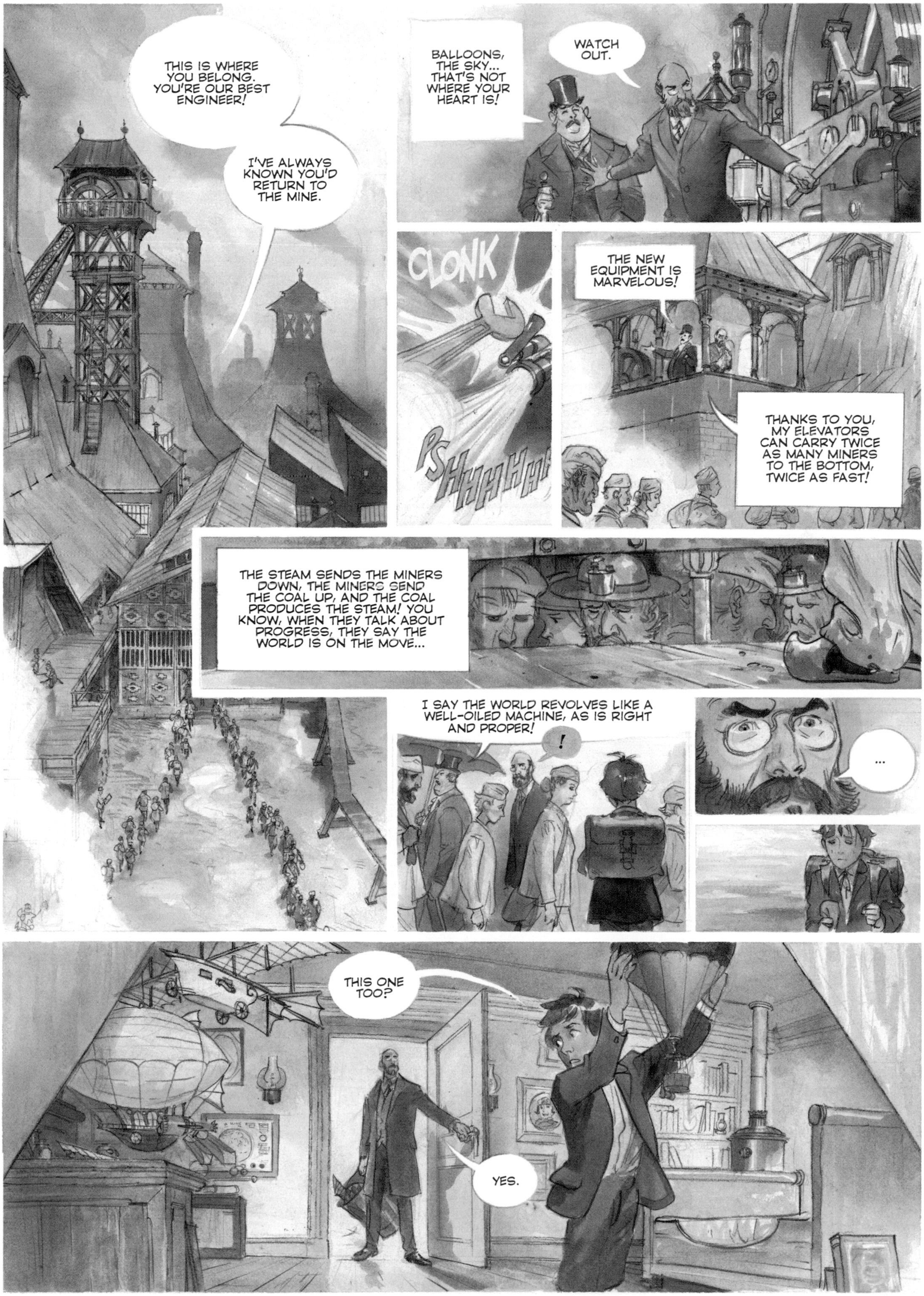
THIS IS WHERE YOU BELONG. YOU'RE OUR BEST ENGINEER!
I'VE ALWAYS KNOWN YOU'D RETURN TO THE MINE.
BALLOONS, THE SKY... THAT'S NOT WHERE YOUR HEART IS!
WATCH OUT.
CLONK
PSHHHHHH
THE NEW EQUIPMENT IS MARVELOUS!
THANKS TO YOU, MY ELEVATORS CAN CARRY TWICE AS MANY MINERS TO THE BOTTOM, TWICE AS FAST!
THE STEAM SENDS THE MINERS DOWN, THE MINERS SEND THE COAL UP, AND THE COAL PRODUCES THE STEAM! YOU KNOW, WHEN THEY TALK ABOUT PROGRESS, THEY SAY THE WORLD IS ON THE MOVE...
I SAY THE WORLD REVOLVES LIKE A WELL-OILED MACHINE, AS IS RIGHT AND PROPER!
!
...
THIS ONE TOO?
YES.

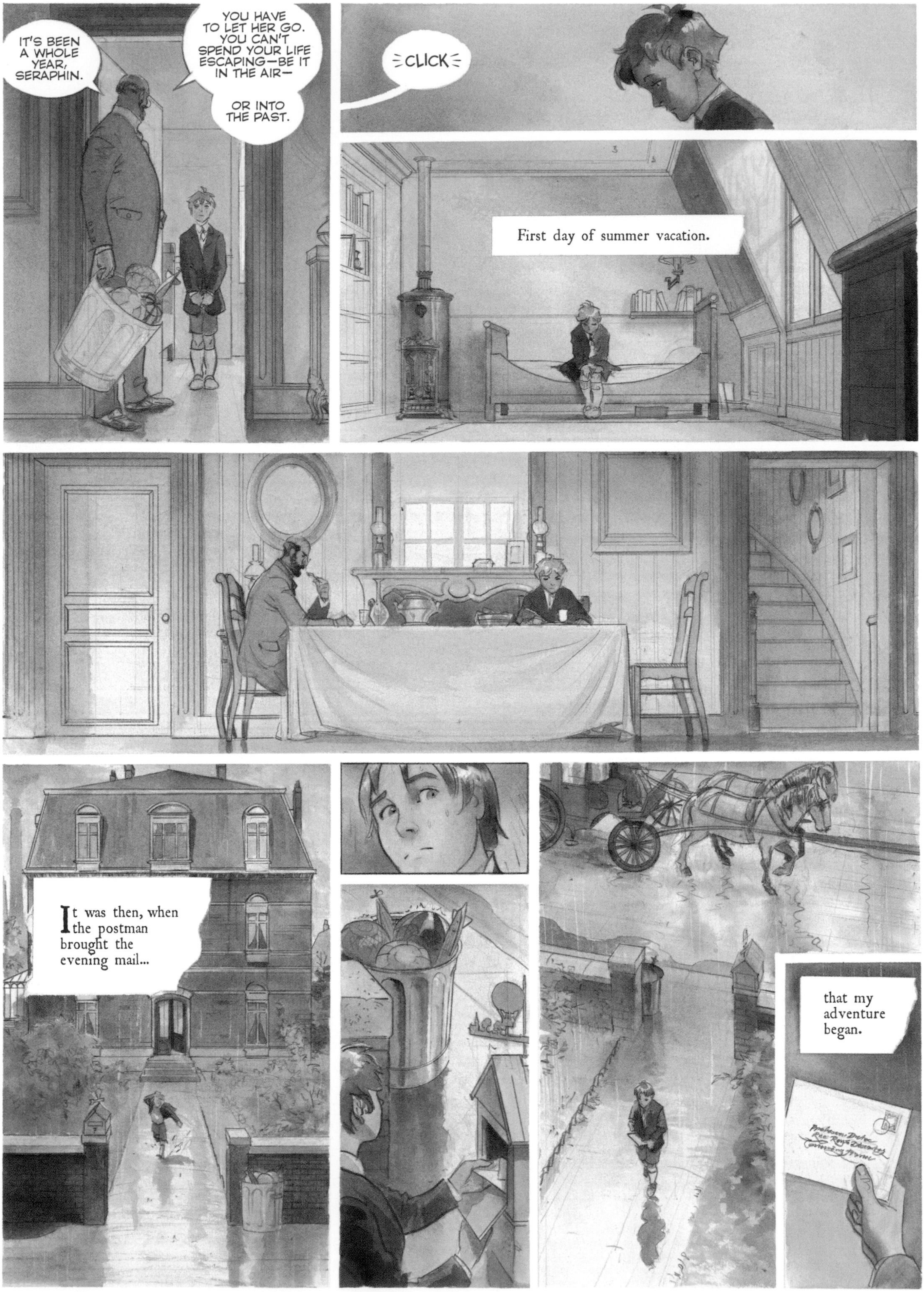

IT'S BEEN A WHOLE YEAR, SERAPHIN.
YOU HAVE TO LET HER GO. YOU CAN'T SPEND YOUR LIFE ESCAPING—BE IT IN THE AIR—
OR INTO THE PAST.
CLICK
First day of summer vacation.
It was then, when the postman brought the evening mail...
that my adventure began.

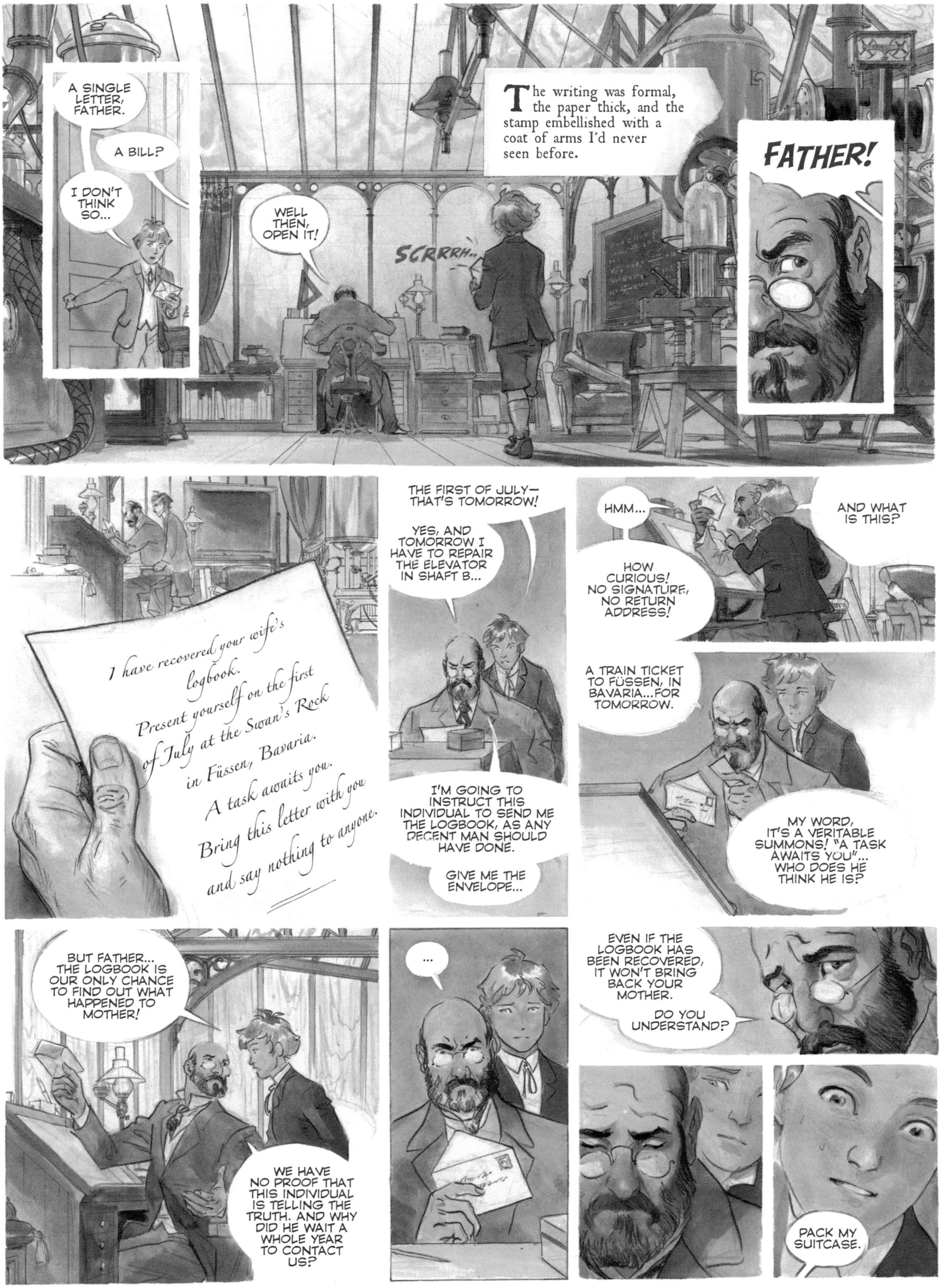

A SINGLE LETTER, FATHER.
A BILL?
I DON'T THINK SO...
The writing was formal, the paper thick, and the stamp embellished with a coat of arms I'd never seen before.
WELL THEN, OPEN IT!
SCRRRH...
FATHER!
I have recovered your wife's logbook. Present yourself on the first of July at the Swan's Rock in Füssen, Bavaria. A task awaits you. Bring this letter with you and say nothing to anyone.
THE FIRST OF JULY—THAT'S TOMORROW!
YES, AND TOMORROW I HAVE TO REPAIR THE ELEVATOR IN SHAFT B...
I'M GOING TO INSTRUCT THIS INDIVIDUAL TO SEND ME THE LOGBOOK, AS ANY DECENT MAN SHOULD HAVE DONE.
GIVE ME THE ENVELOPE...
HMM...
AND WHAT IS THIS?
HOW CURIOUS! NO SIGNATURE, NO RETURN ADDRESS!
A TRAIN TICKET TO FÜSSEN, IN BAVARIA...FOR TOMORROW.
MY WORD, IT'S A VERITABLE SUMMONS! "A TASK AWAITS YOU"... WHO DOES HE THINK HE IS?
BUT FATHER... THE LOGBOOK IS OUR ONLY CHANCE TO FIND OUT WHAT HAPPENED TO MOTHER!
WE HAVE NO PROOF THAT THIS INDIVIDUAL IS TELLING THE TRUTH. AND WHY DID HE WAIT A WHOLE YEAR TO CONTACT US?
...
EVEN IF THE LOGBOOK HAS BEEN RECOVERED, IT WON'T BRING BACK YOUR MOTHER.
DO YOU UNDERSTAND?
PACK MY SUITCASE.

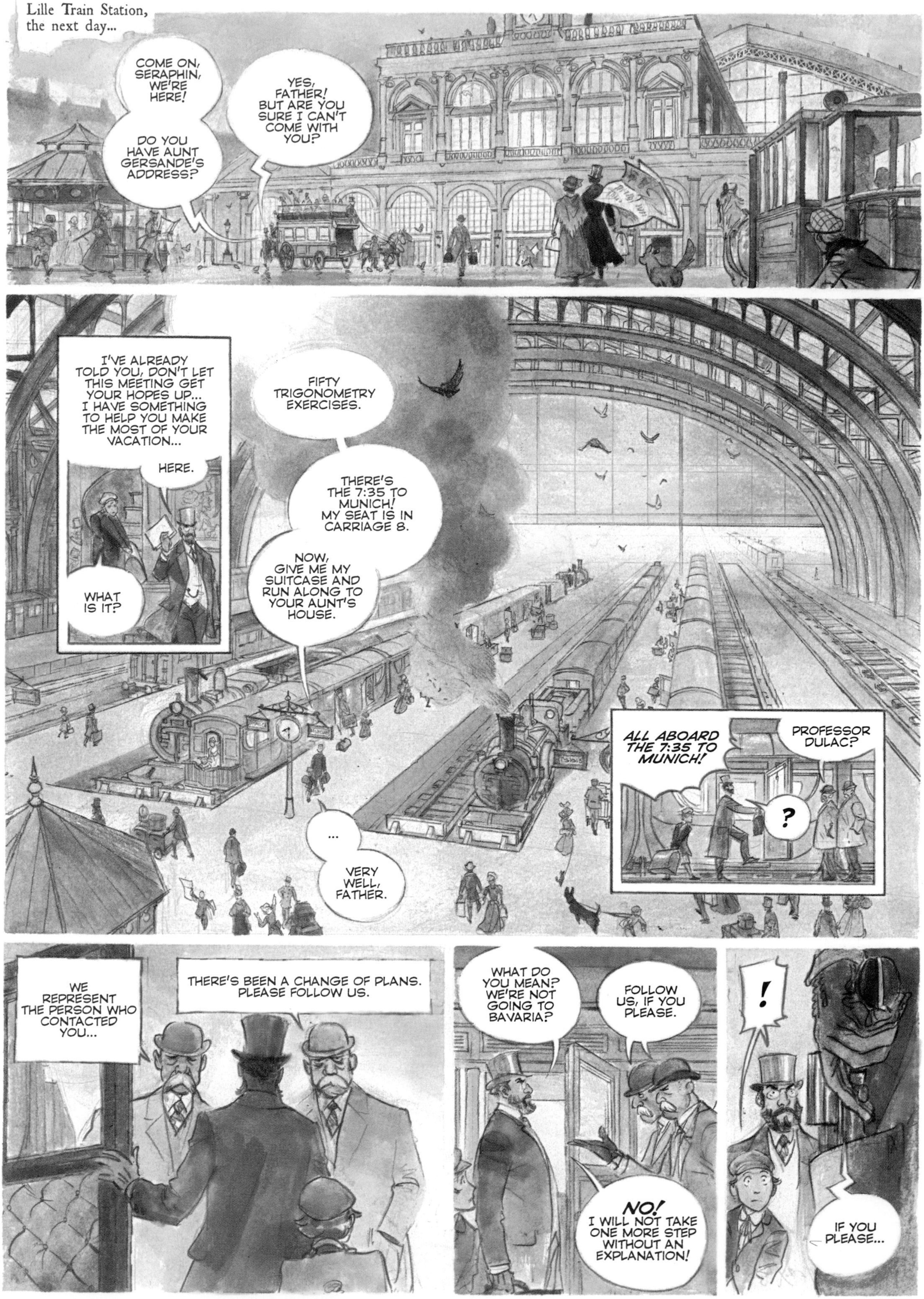
Lille Train Station, the next day...
COME ON, SERAPHIN, WE'RE HERE!
DO YOU HAVE AUNT GERSANDE'S ADDRESS?
YES, FATHER! BUT ARE YOU SURE I CAN'T COME WITH YOU?
I'VE ALREADY TOLD YOU, DON'T LET THIS MEETING GET YOUR HOPES UP... I HAVE SOMETHING TO HELP YOU MAKE THE MOST OF YOUR VACATION...
HERE.
WHAT IS IT?
FIFTY TRIGONOMETRY EXERCISES.
THERE'S THE 7:35 TO MUNICH! MY SEAT IS IN CARRIAGE 8.
NOW, GIVE ME MY SUITCASE AND RUN ALONG TO YOUR AUNT'S HOUSE.
...
VERY WELL, FATHER.
ALL ABOARD THE 7:35 TO MUNICH!
PROFESSOR DULAC?
?
WE REPRESENT THE PERSON WHO CONTACTED YOU...
THERE'S BEEN A CHANGE OF PLANS. PLEASE FOLLOW US.
WHAT DO YOU MEAN? WE'RE NOT GOING TO BAVARIA?
FOLLOW US, IF YOU PLEASE.
NO! I WILL NOT TAKE ONE MORE STEP WITHOUT AN EXPLANATION!
!
IF YOU PLEASE...

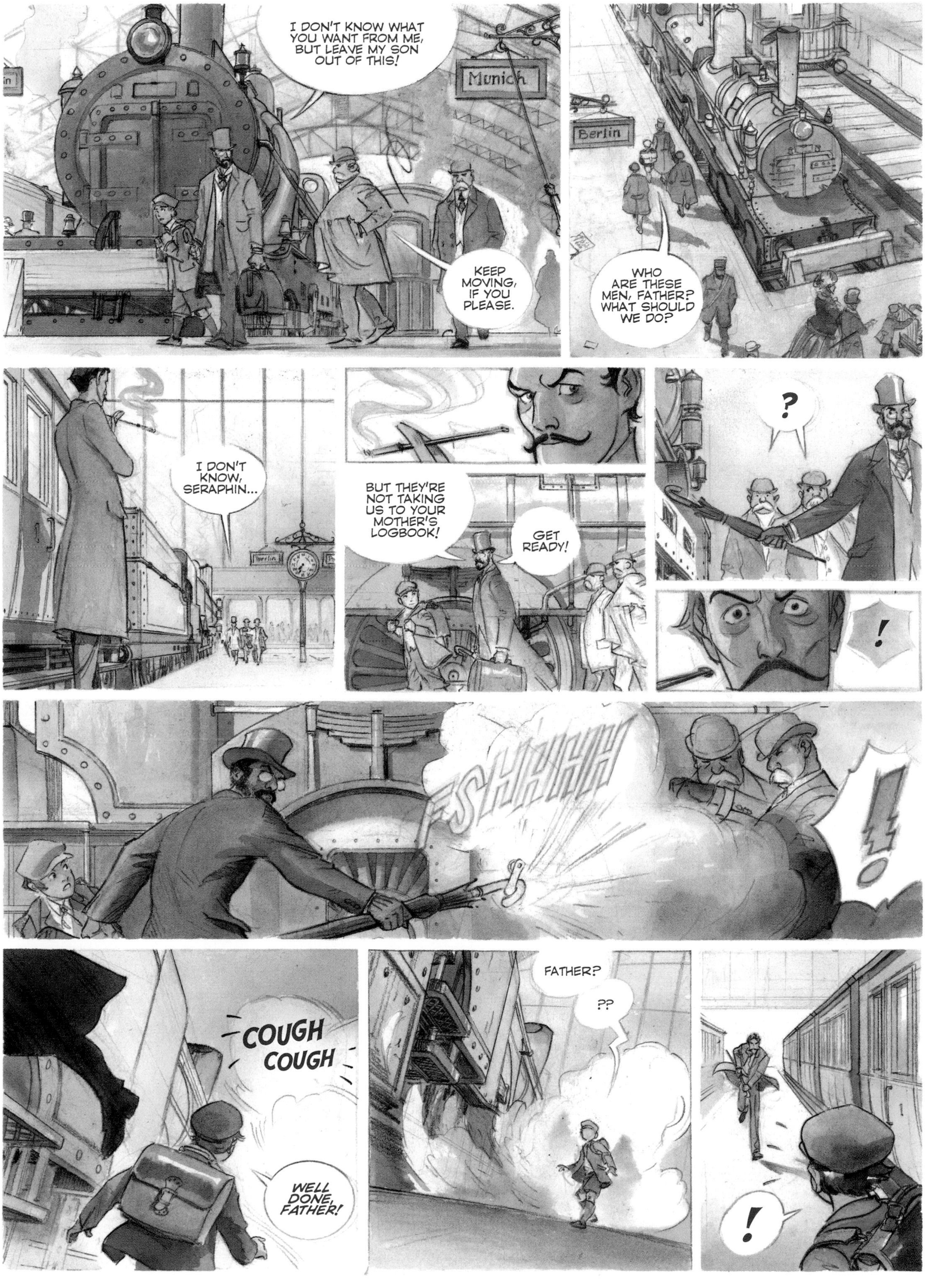
Berlin
I DON'T KNOW WHAT YOU WANT FROM ME, BUT LEAVE MY SON OUT OF THIS!
Munich
KEEP MOVING, IF YOU PLEASE.
Berlin
WHO ARE THESE MEN, FATHER? WHAT SHOULD WE DO?
I DON'T KNOW, SERAPHIN...
BUT THEY'RE NOT TAKING US TO YOUR MOTHER'S LOGBOOK!
GET READY!
?
!
FSHHHHH
!
COUGH
COUGH
WELL DONE, FATHER!
FATHER?
??
!

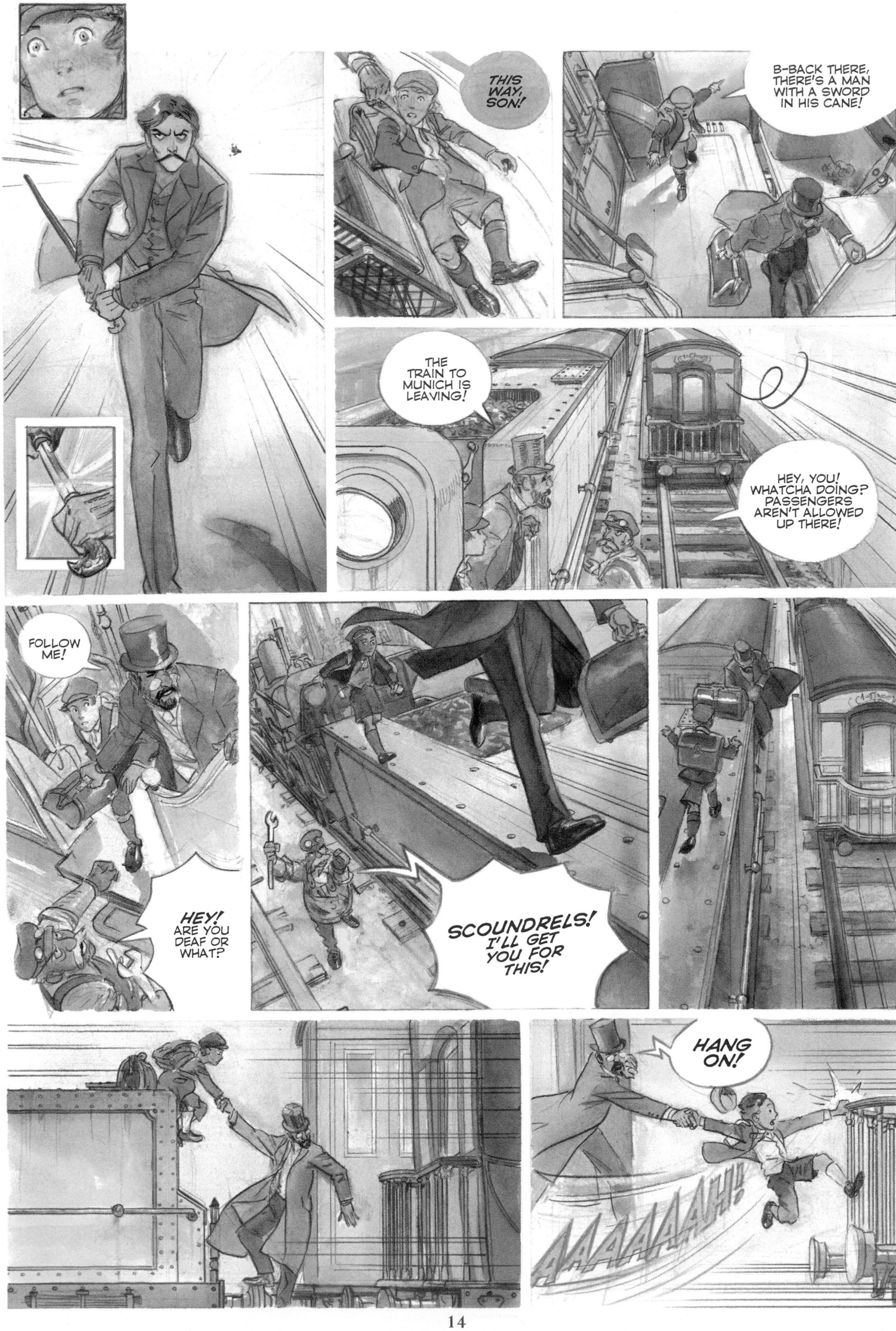
THIS WAY, SON!
B-BACK THERE, THERE'S A MAN WITH A SWORD IN HIS CANE!
THE TRAIN TO MUNICH IS LEAVING!
HEY, YOU! WHATCHA DOING? PASSENGERS AREN'T ALLOWED UP THERE!
FOLLOW ME!
HEY! ARE YOU DEAF OR WHAT?
SCOUNDRELS! I'LL GET YOU FOR THIS!
HANG ON!
AAAAAAAH!!

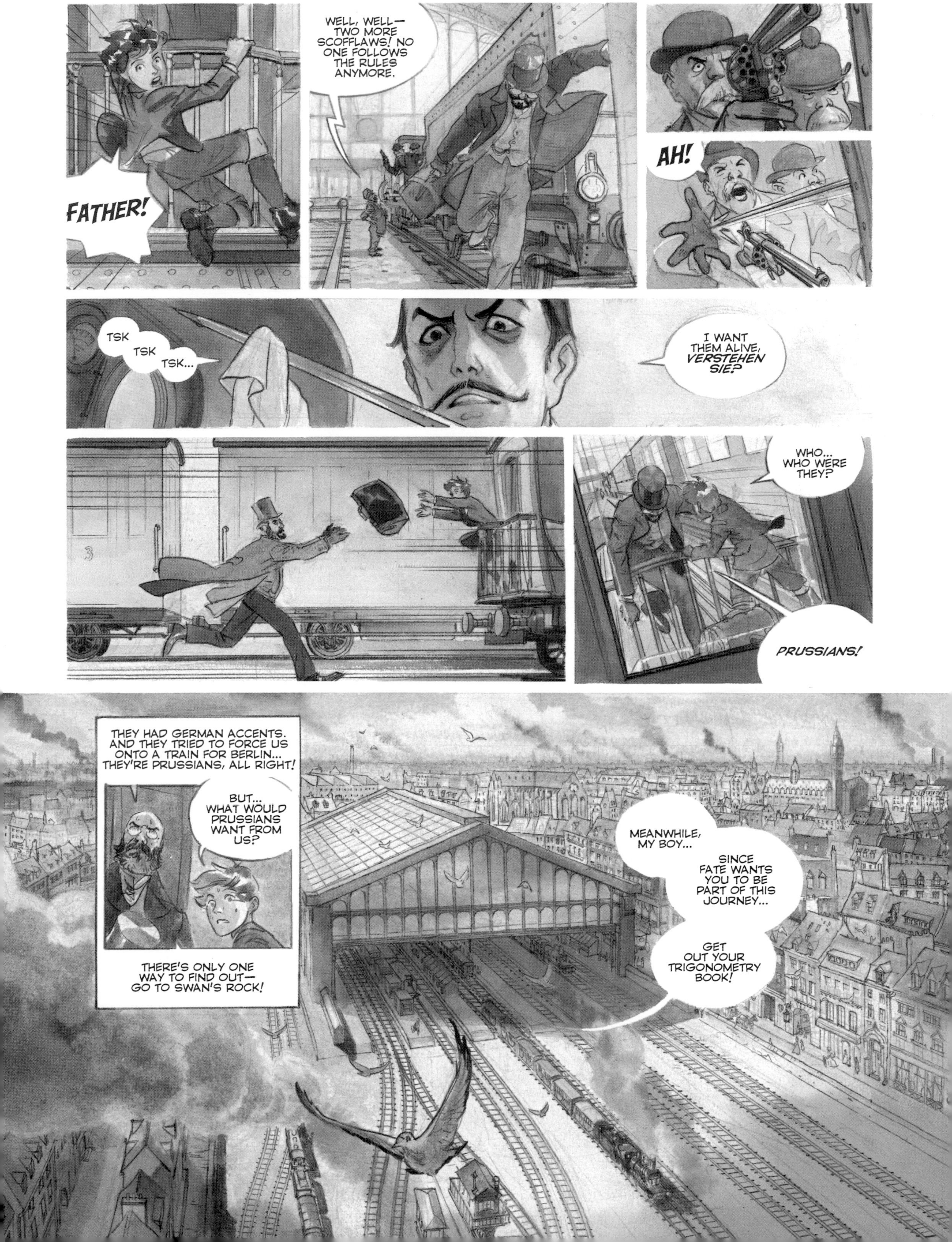
FATHER!
WELL, WELL— TWO MORE SCOFFLAWS! NO ONE FOLLOWS THE RULES ANYMORE.
AH!
TSK
TSK
TSK...
I WANT THEM ALIVE, VERSTEHEN SIE?
WHO... WHO WERE THEY?
PRUSSIANS!
THEY HAD GERMAN ACCENTS. AND THEY TRIED TO FORCE US ONTO A TRAIN FOR BERLIN... THEY'RE PRUSSIANS, ALL RIGHT!
BUT... WHAT WOULD PRUSSIANS WANT FROM US?
THERE'S ONLY ONE WAY TO FIND OUT— GO TO SWAN'S ROCK!
MEANWHILE, MY BOY...
SINCE FATE WANTS YOU TO BE PART OF THIS JOURNEY...
GET OUT YOUR TRIGONOMETRY BOOK!

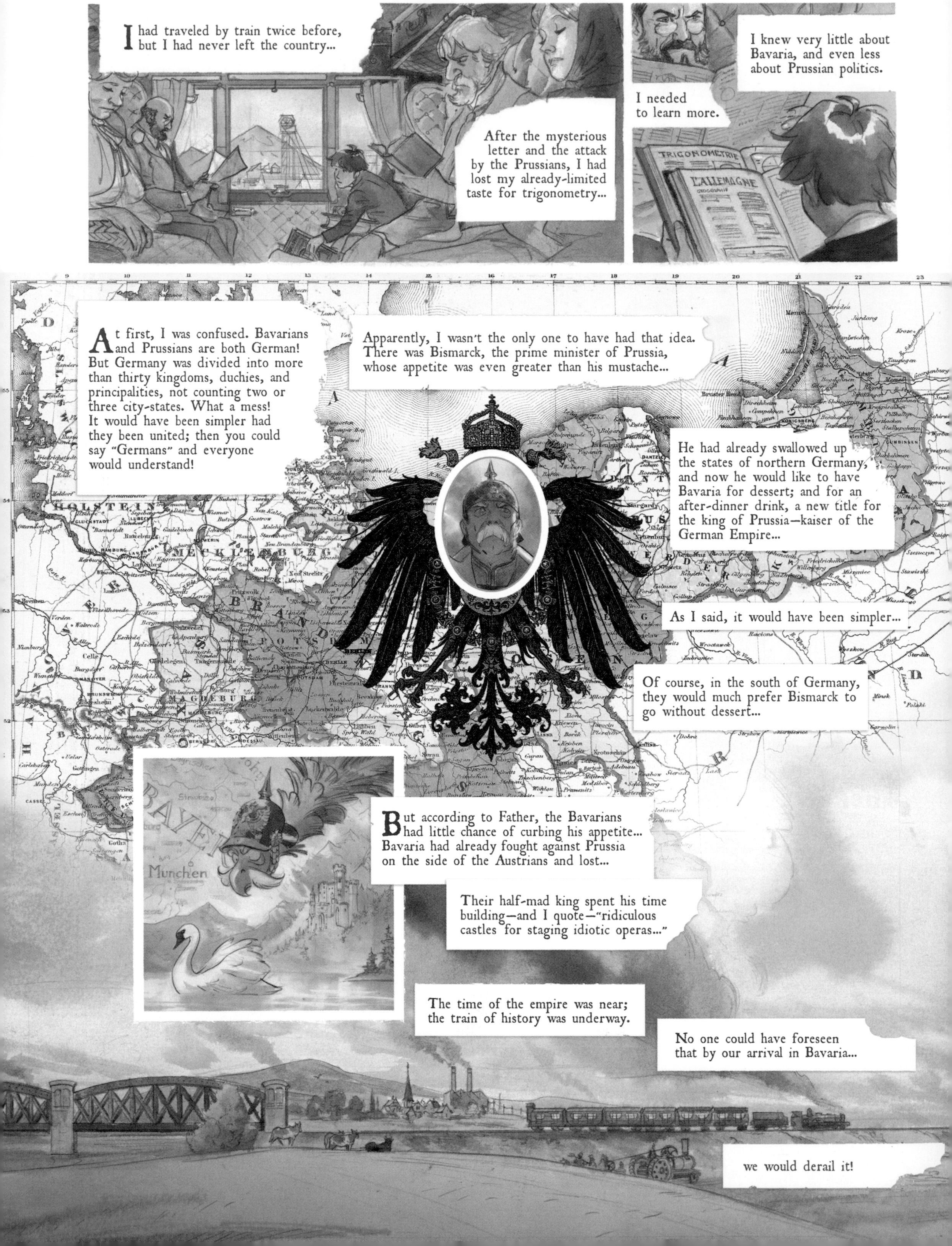

I had traveled by train twice before, but I had never left the country...
After the mysterious letter and the attack by the Prussians, I had lost my already-limited taste for trigonometry...
I knew very little about Bavaria, and even less about Prussian politics.
I needed to learn more.
TRIGONOMETRIE
L'ALLEMAGNE
At first, I was confused. Bavarians and Prussians are both German! But Germany was divided into more than thirty kingdoms, duchies, and principalities, not counting two or three city-states. What a mess! It would have been simpler had they been united; then you could say "Germans" and everyone would understand!
Apparently, I wasn't the only one to have had that idea. There was Bismarck, the prime minister of Prussia, whose appetite was even greater than his mustache...
He had already swallowed up the states of northern Germany, and now he would like to have Bavaria for dessert; and for an after-dinner drink, a new title for the king of Prussia—kaiser of the German Empire...
As I said, it would have been simpler...
Of course, in the south of Germany, they would much prefer Bismarck to go without dessert...
But according to Father, the Bavarians had little chance of curbing his appetite... Bavaria had already fought against Prussia on the side of the Austrians and lost...
Their half-mad king spent his time building—and I quote—"ridiculous castles for staging idiotic operas..."
The time of the empire was near; the train of history was underway.
No one could have foreseen that by our arrival in Bavaria...
we would derail it!

A SNACK, LADIES AND GENTLEMEN? SAUSAGES? PRETZELS?

AH, WE'RE GETTING CLOSE TO THE BORDER!

WHAT'S A PRETZEL?

TRY ONE!

I'VE JUST ABOUT GONE BLIND STUDYING THIS MAP, BUT I STILL DON'T UNDERSTAND WHAT THE PRUSSIANS WANT FROM US!

SO THERE'S A MAP OF EUROPE IN YOUR TRIGONOMETRY BOOK?

I'VE BEEN THINKING... YOUR MOTHER'S LOGBOOK HASN'T FALLEN INTO JUST ANYONE'S HANDS. WHOEVER SENT US THAT LETTER MUST HAVE BEEN UNDER PRUSSIAN SURVEILLANCE...

BUT WHO IS HE, AND WHY THE MYSTERY?

GULP

I DON'T KNOW, SERAPHIN...

L ater in the day, we finally passed the borders of France into the grand duchy of Baden, then the kingdom of Württemberg and the province of Hohenzollern.

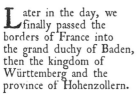

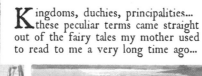

K ingdoms, duchies, principalities... these peculiar terms came straight out of the fairy tales my mother used to read to me a very long time ago...

PRETZEL, YOUNG MAN?

Finally, we entered Bavaria...

PRETZEL?

UM...

A s the train crossed an endless forest, it seemed to me that we were going backward in time. Trains were more dilapidated. Telegraph poles became scarcer, then disappeared. No more chimneys, no more factories...

And finally...

No more trains.

SWAN'S ROCK? FOLLOW THIS ROAD THREE KILOMETERS TO THE END...BUT WHAT ARE YOU GOING TO DO THERE AT THIS TIME OF DAY?

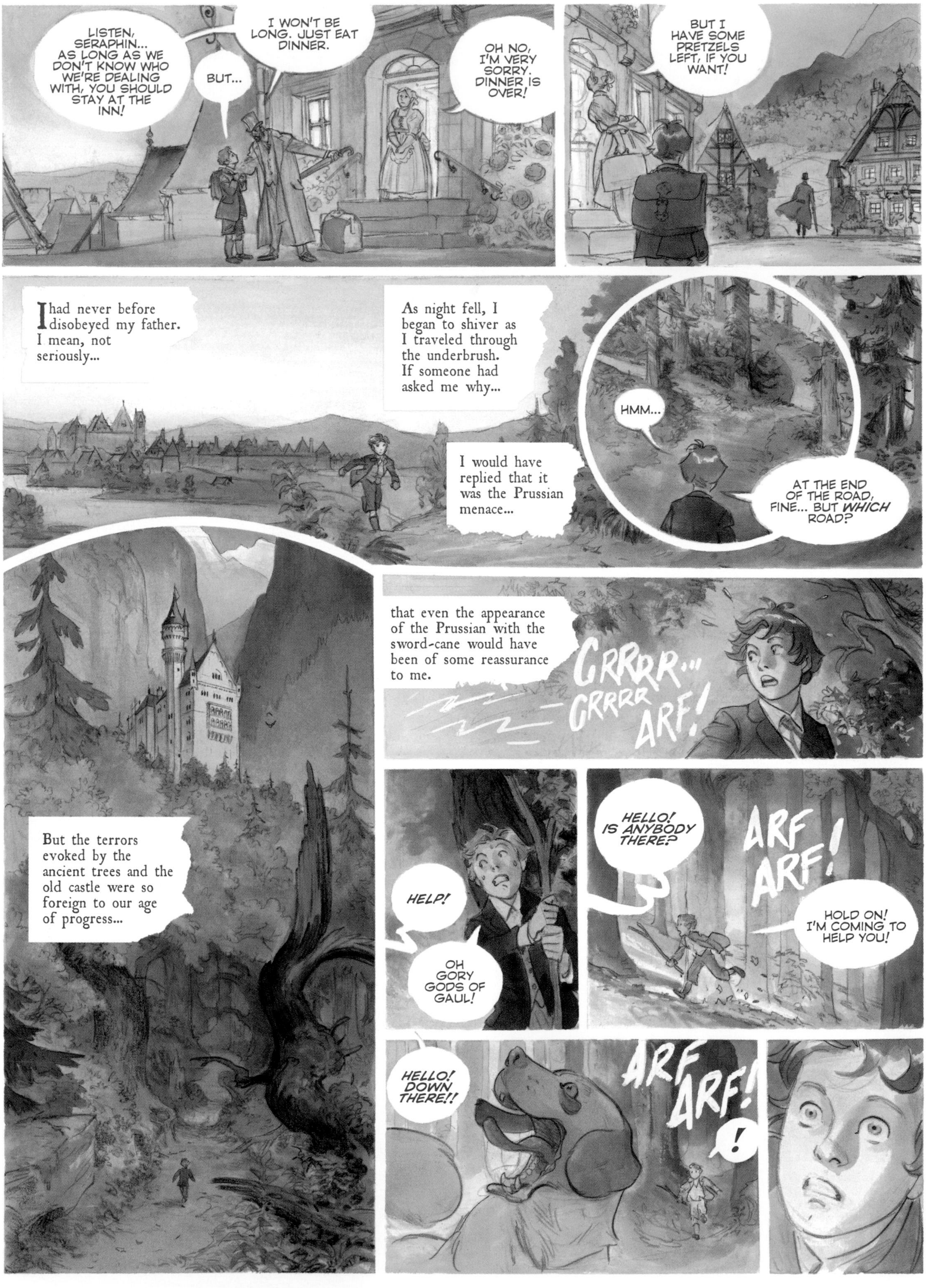

LISTEN, SERAPHIN... AS LONG AS WE DON'T KNOW WHO WE'RE DEALING WITH, YOU SHOULD STAY AT THE INN!
BUT...
I WON'T BE LONG. JUST EAT DINNER.
OH NO, I'M VERY SORRY. DINNER IS OVER!
BUT I HAVE SOME PRETZELS LEFT, IF YOU WANT!
I had never before disobeyed my father. I mean, not seriously...
As night fell, I began to shiver as I traveled through the underbrush. If someone had asked me why...
I would have replied that it was the Prussian menace...
HMM...
AT THE END OF THE ROAD, FINE... BUT WHICH ROAD?
But the terrors evoked by the ancient trees and the old castle were so foreign to our age of progress...
that even the appearance of the Prussian with the sword-cane would have been of some reassurance to me.
GRRRR... GRRRR ARF!
HELP!
OH GORY GODS OF GAUL!
HELLO! IS ANYBODY THERE?
ARF ARF!
HOLD ON! I'M COMING TO HELP YOU!
HELLO! DOWN THERE!!
ARF ARF!
!

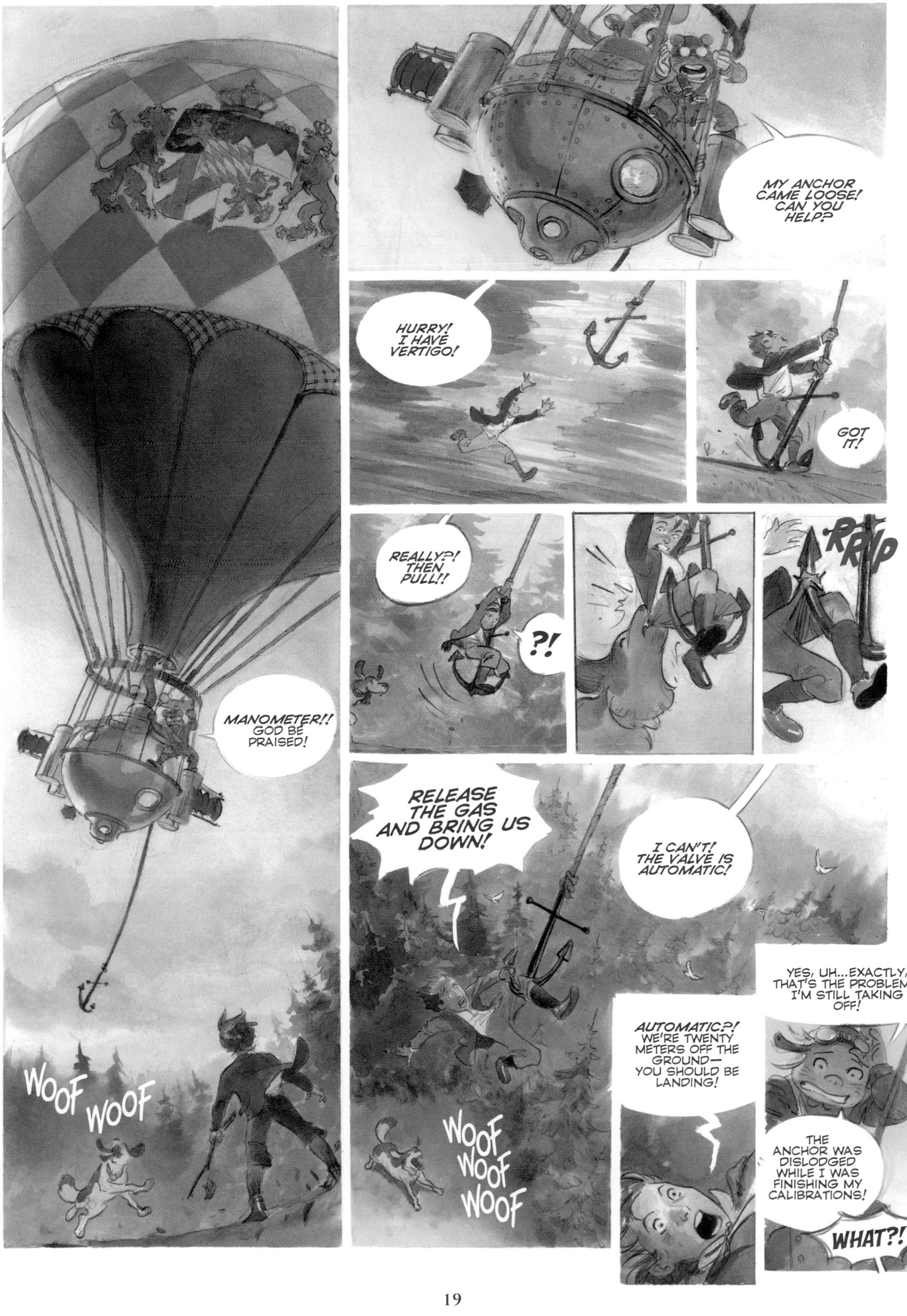
MY ANCHOR CAME LOOSE! CAN YOU HELP?
MANOMETER!! GOD BE PRAISED!
WOOF WOOF
HURRY! I HAVE VERTIGO!
GOT IT!
REALLY?! THEN PULL!!
?!
RRIP
RELEASE THE GAS AND BRING US DOWN!
I CAN'T! THE VALVE IS AUTOMATIC!
WOOF WOOF WOOF
AUTOMATIC?! WE'RE TWENTY METERS OFF THE GROUND— YOU SHOULD BE LANDING!
YES, UH...EXACTLY, THAT'S THE PROBLEM... I'M STILL TAKING OFF!
THE ANCHOR WAS DISLODGED WHILE I WAS FINISHING MY CALIBRATIONS!
WHAT?!

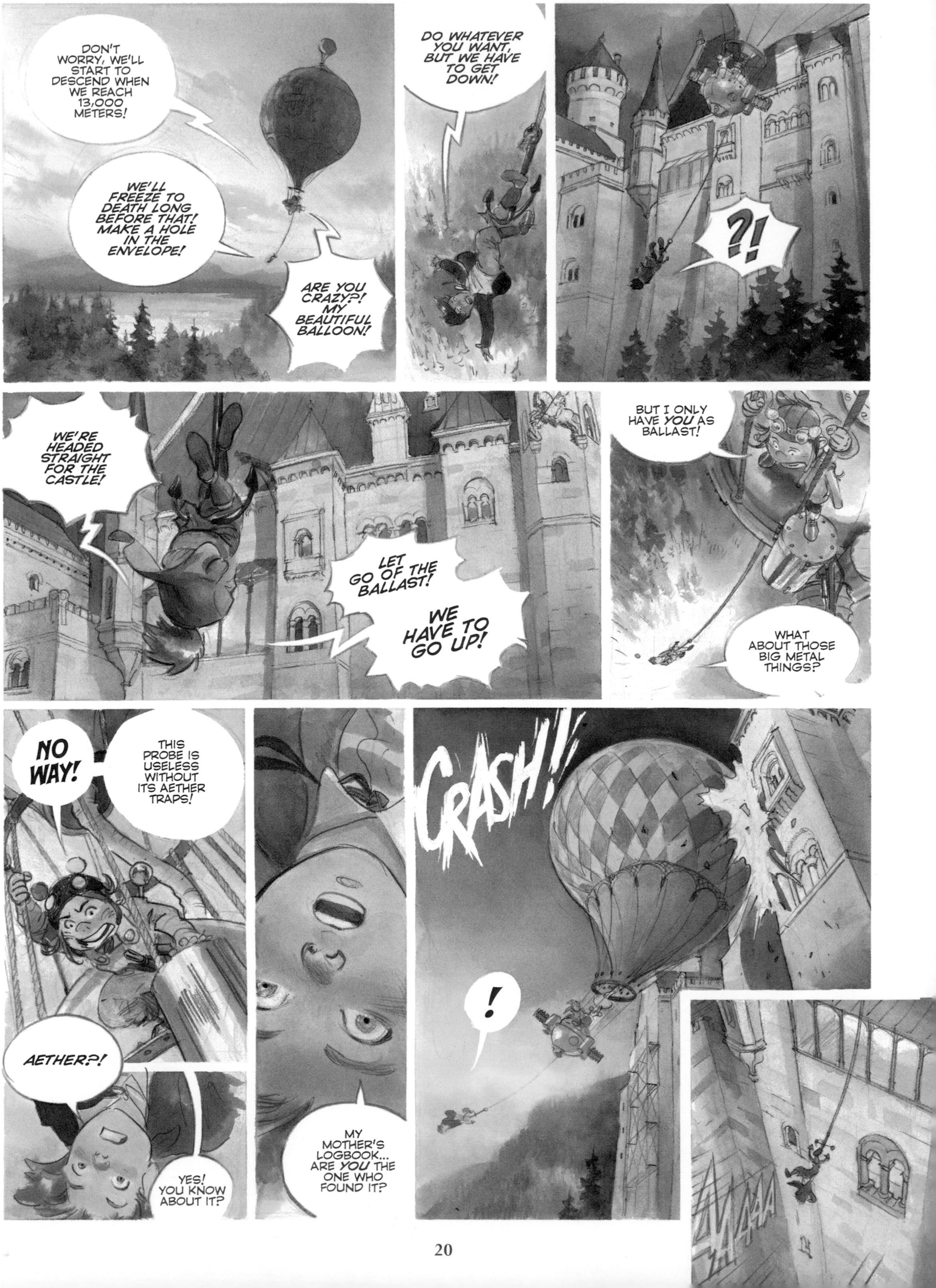
DON'T WORRY, WE'LL START TO DESCEND WHEN WE REACH 13,000 METERS!
WE'LL FREEZE TO DEATH LONG BEFORE THAT! MAKE A HOLE IN THE ENVELOPE!
ARE YOU CRAZY?! MY BEAUTIFUL BALLOON!
DO WHATEVER YOU WANT, BUT WE HAVE TO GET DOWN!
?!
WE'RE HEADED STRAIGHT FOR THE CASTLE!
LET GO OF THE BALLAST!
WE HAVE TO GO UP!
BUT I ONLY HAVE YOU AS BALLAST!
WHAT ABOUT THOSE BIG METAL THINGS?
NO WAY!
THIS PROBE IS USELESS WITHOUT ITS AETHER TRAPS!
AETHER?!
YES! YOU KNOW ABOUT IT?
MY MOTHER'S LOGBOOK... ARE YOU THE ONE WHO FOUND IT?
CRASH!!
!

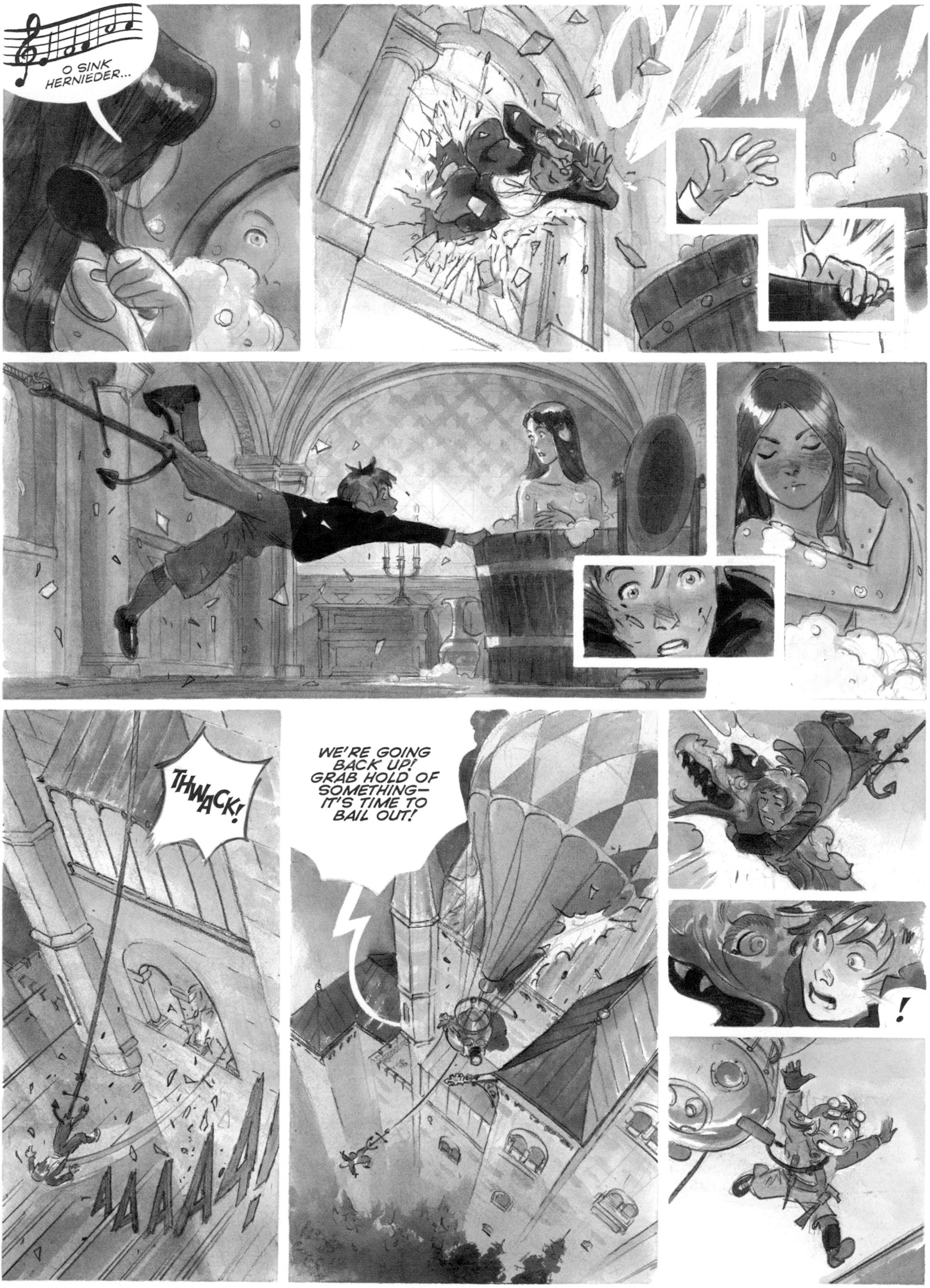
O SINK HERNIEDER...
CLANG!
THWACK!
AAAAA!
WE'RE GOING BACK UP! GRAB HOLD OF SOMETHING— IT'S TIME TO BAIL OUT!
!

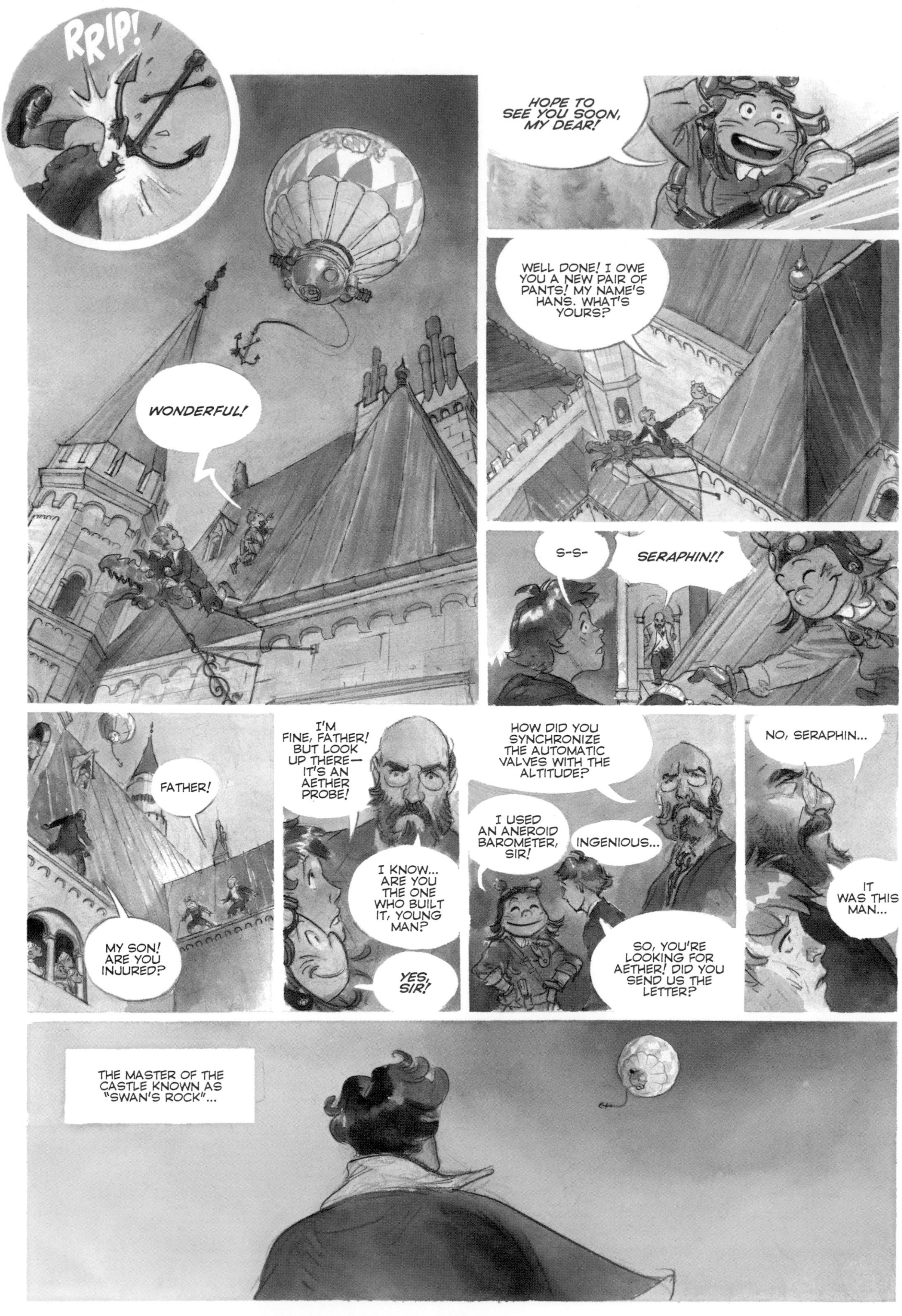
RRIP!
WONDERFUL!
HOPE TO SEE YOU SOON, MY DEAR!
WELL DONE! I OWE YOU A NEW PAIR OF PANTS! MY NAME'S HANS. WHAT'S YOURS?
S-S-
SERAPHIN!!
FATHER!
MY SON! ARE YOU INJURED?
I'M FINE, FATHER! BUT LOOK UP THERE— IT'S AN AETHER PROBE!
I KNOW... ARE YOU THE ONE WHO BUILT IT, YOUNG MAN?
YES, SIR!
HOW DID YOU SYNCHRONIZE THE AUTOMATIC VALVES WITH THE ALTITUDE?
I USED AN ANEROID BAROMETER, SIR!
INGENIOUS...
SO, YOU'RE LOOKING FOR AETHER! DID YOU SEND US THE LETTER?
NO, SERAPHIN...
IT WAS THIS MAN...
THE MASTER OF THE CASTLE KNOWN AS "SWAN'S ROCK"...

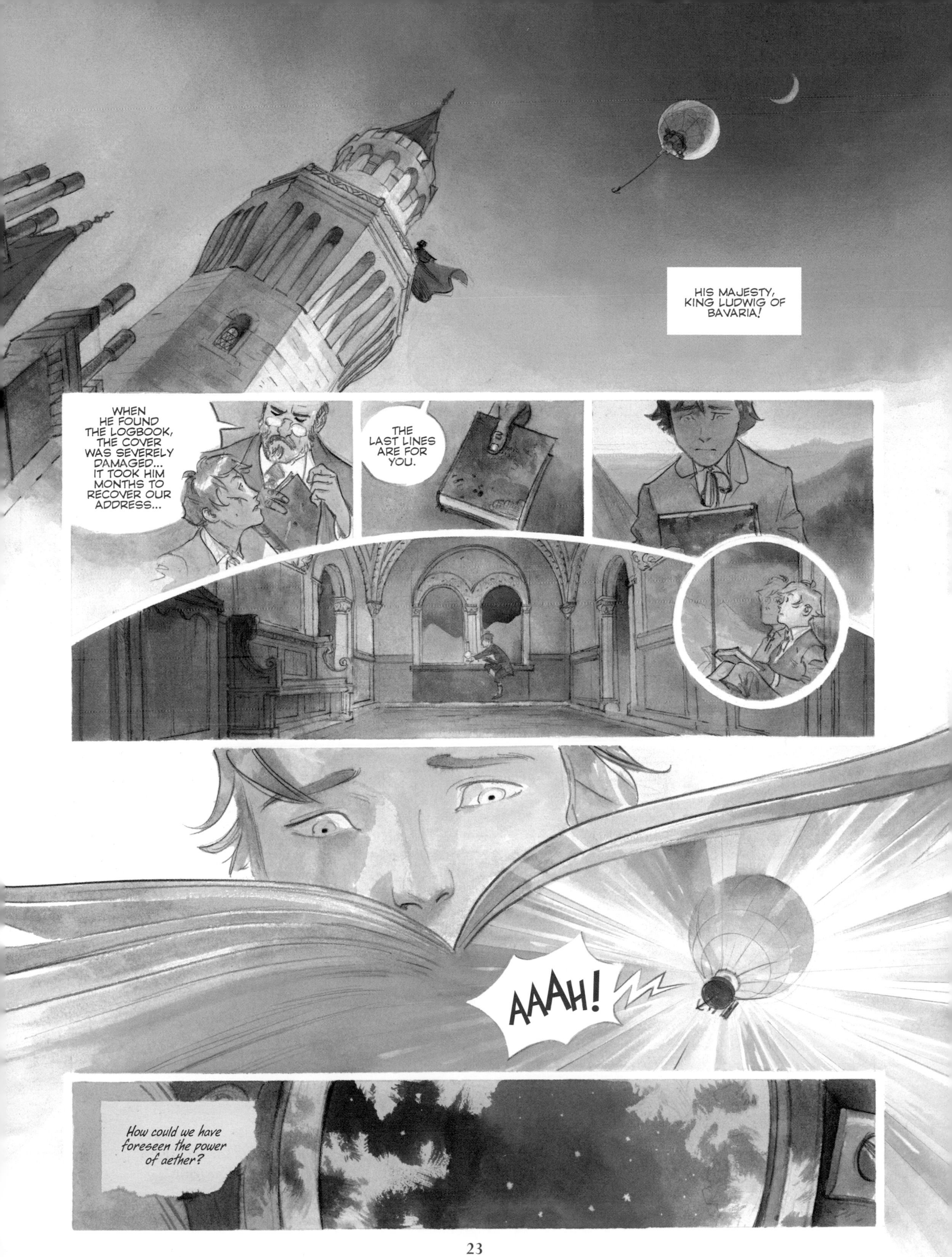
HIS MAJESTY, KING LUDWIG OF BAVARIA!
WHEN HE FOUND THE LOGBOOK, THE COVER WAS SEVERELY DAMAGED... IT TOOK HIM MONTHS TO RECOVER OUR ADDRESS...
THE LAST LINES ARE FOR YOU.
AAAH!
How could we have foreseen the power of aether?

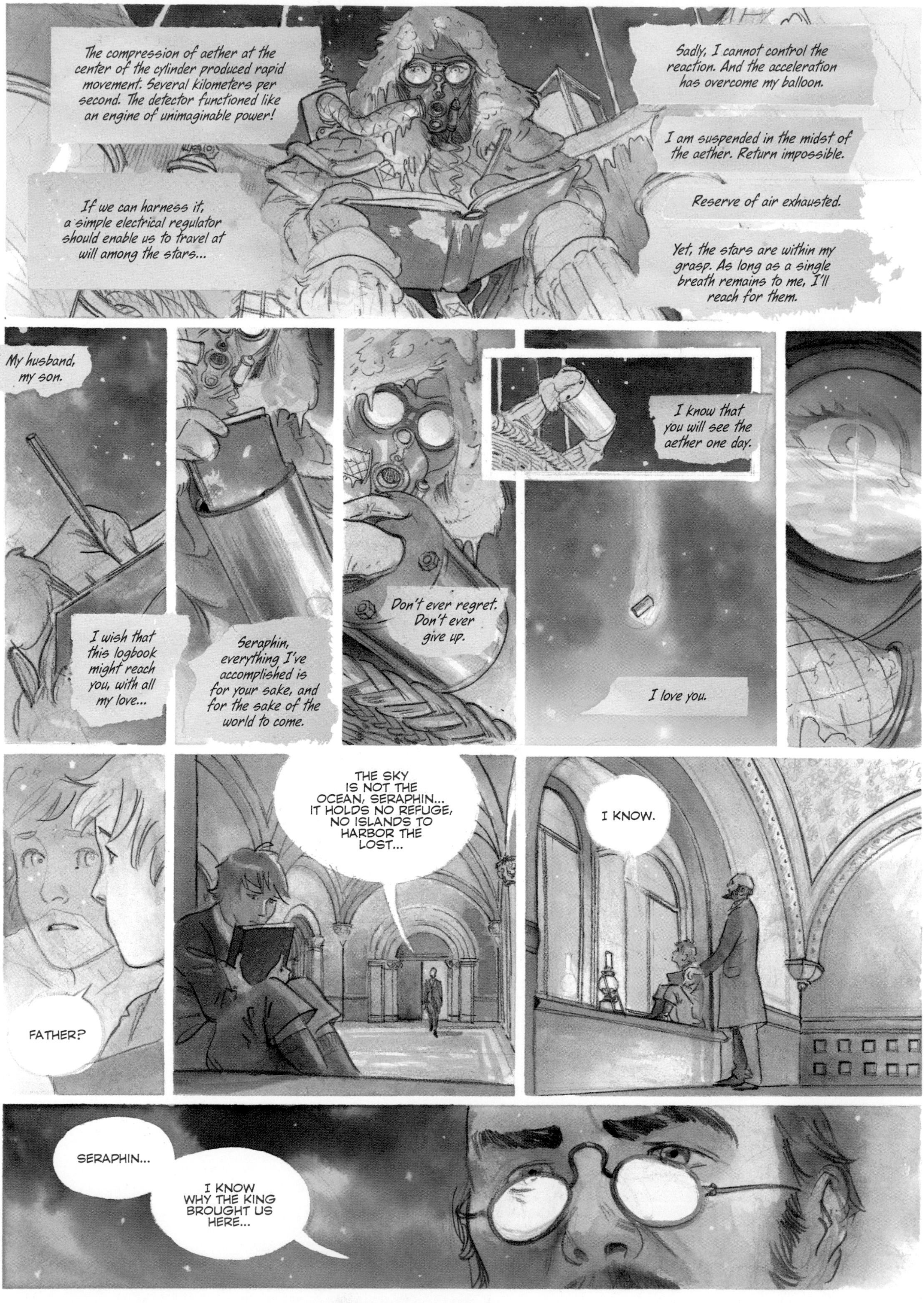
The compression of aether at the center of the cylinder produced rapid movement. Several kilometers per second. The detector functioned like an engine of unimaginable power!
If we can harness it, a simple electrical regulator should enable us to travel at will among the stars...
Sadly, I cannot control the reaction. And the acceleration has overcome my balloon.
I am suspended in the midst of the aether. Return impossible.
Reserve of air exhausted.
Yet, the stars are within my grasp. As long as a single breath remains to me, I'll reach for them.
My husband, my son.
I wish that this logbook might reach you, with all my love...
Seraphin, everything I've accomplished is for your sake, and for the sake of the world to come.
Don't ever regret. Don't ever give up.
I know that you will see the aether one day.
I love you.
FATHER?
THE SKY IS NOT THE OCEAN, SERAPHIN... IT HOLDS NO REFUGE, NO ISLANDS TO HARBOR THE LOST...
I KNOW.
SERAPHIN...
I KNOW WHY THE KING BROUGHT US HERE...

CHAPTER 2

THE KNIGHTS OF AETHER

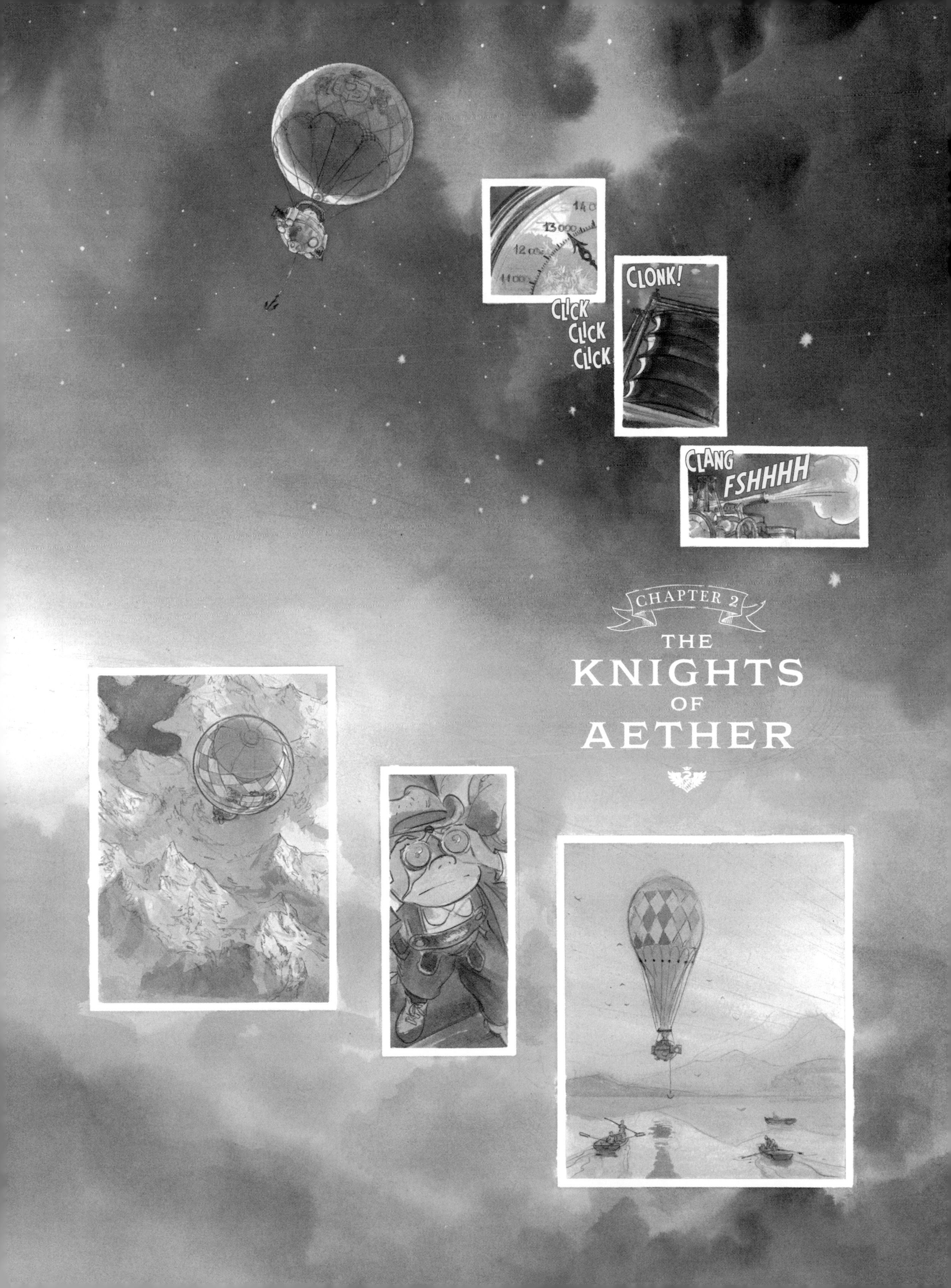
CLICK
CLICK
CLICK
CLONK!
CLANG
FSHHHH

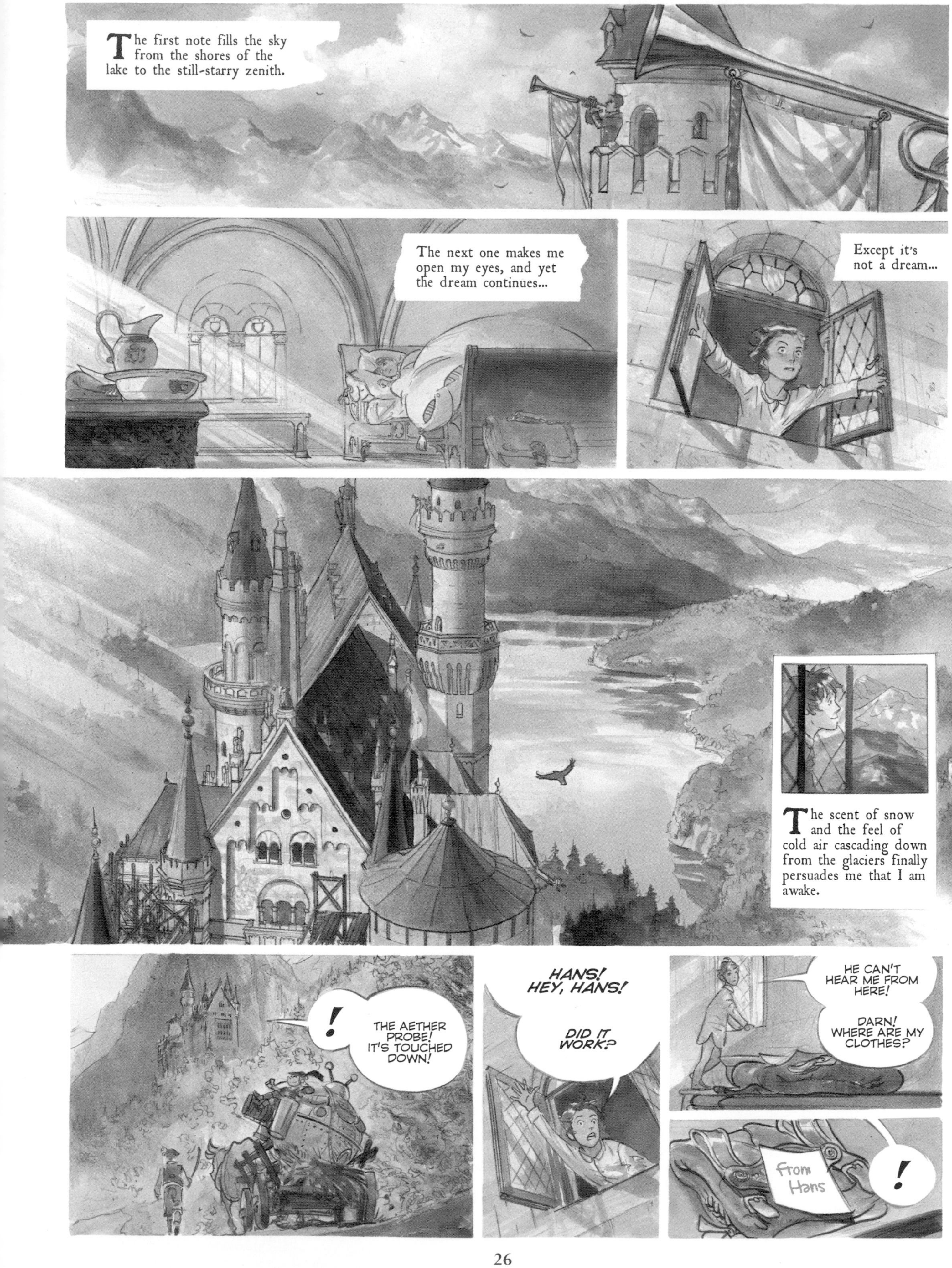
The first note fills the sky from the shores of the lake to the still-starry zenith.
The next one makes me open my eyes, and yet the dream continues...
Except it's not a dream...
The scent of snow and the feel of cold air cascading down from the glaciers finally persuades me that I am awake.
!
THE AETHER PROBE! IT'S TOUCHED DOWN!
HANS! HEY, HANS!
DID IT WORK?
HE CAN'T HEAR ME FROM HERE!
DARN! WHERE ARE MY CLOTHES?
From Hans
!

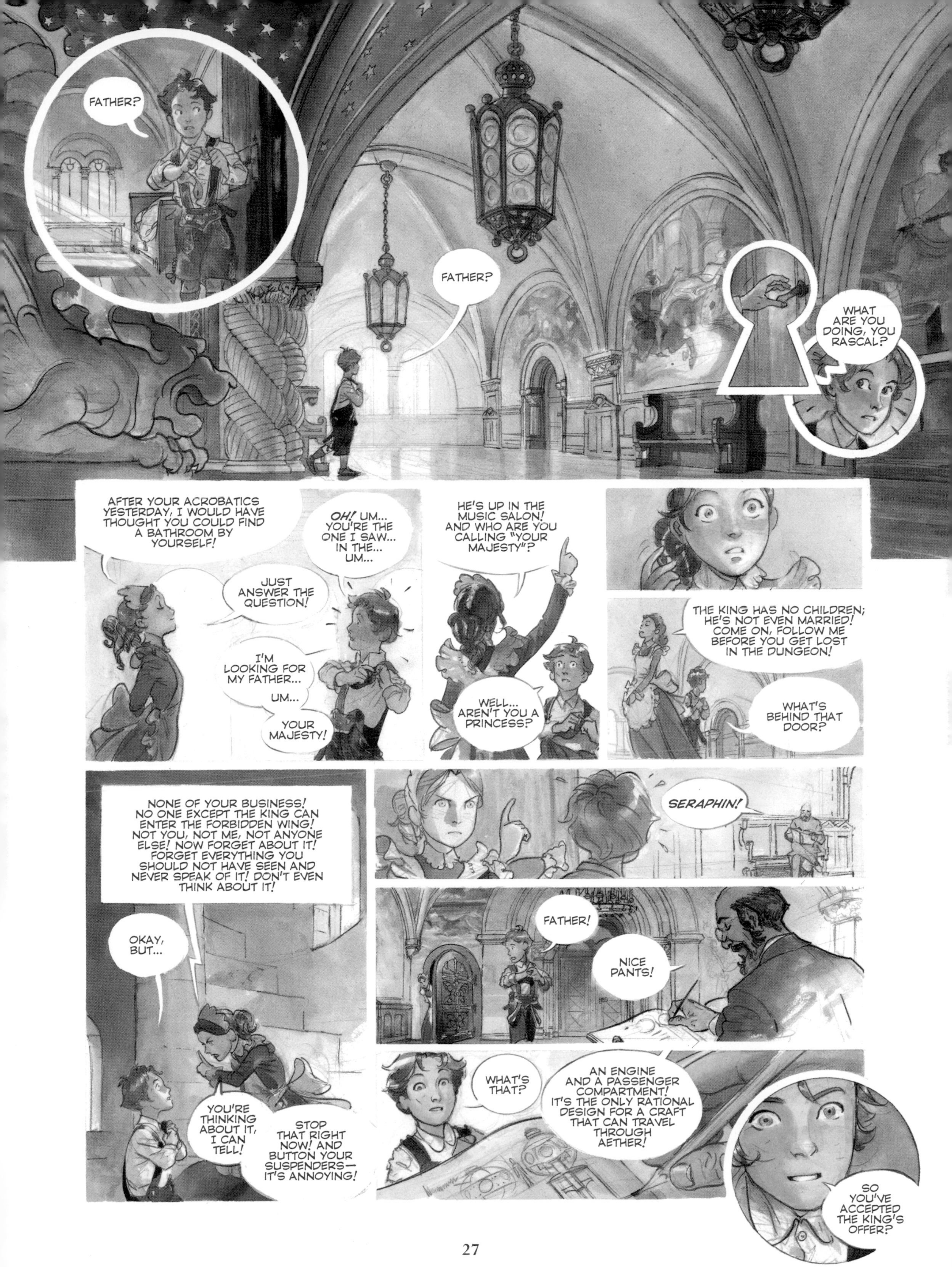
FATHER?
FATHER?
WHAT ARE YOU DOING, YOU RASCAL?
AFTER YOUR ACROBATICS YESTERDAY, I WOULD HAVE THOUGHT YOU COULD FIND A BATHROOM BY YOURSELF!
OH! UM... YOU'RE THE ONE I SAW... IN THE... UM...
JUST ANSWER THE QUESTION!
I'M LOOKING FOR MY FATHER...
UM...
YOUR MAJESTY!
HE'S UP IN THE MUSIC SALON! AND WHO ARE YOU CALLING "YOUR MAJESTY"?
WELL... AREN'T YOU A PRINCESS?
THE KING HAS NO CHILDREN; HE'S NOT EVEN MARRIED! COME ON, FOLLOW ME BEFORE YOU GET LOST IN THE DUNGEON!
WHAT'S BEHIND THAT DOOR?
NONE OF YOUR BUSINESS! NO ONE EXCEPT THE KING CAN ENTER THE FORBIDDEN WING! NOT YOU, NOT ME, NOT ANYONE ELSE! NOW FORGET ABOUT IT! FORGET EVERYTHING YOU SHOULD NOT HAVE SEEN AND NEVER SPEAK OF IT! DON'T EVEN THINK ABOUT IT!
OKAY, BUT...
YOU'RE THINKING ABOUT IT, I CAN TELL!
STOP THAT RIGHT NOW! AND BUTTON YOUR SUSPENDERS— IT'S ANNOYING!
SERAPHIN!
FATHER!
NICE PANTS!
WHAT'S THAT?
AN ENGINE AND A PASSENGER COMPARTMENT! IT'S THE ONLY RATIONAL DESIGN FOR A CRAFT THAT CAN TRAVEL THROUGH AETHER!
SO YOU'VE ACCEPTED THE KING'S OFFER?

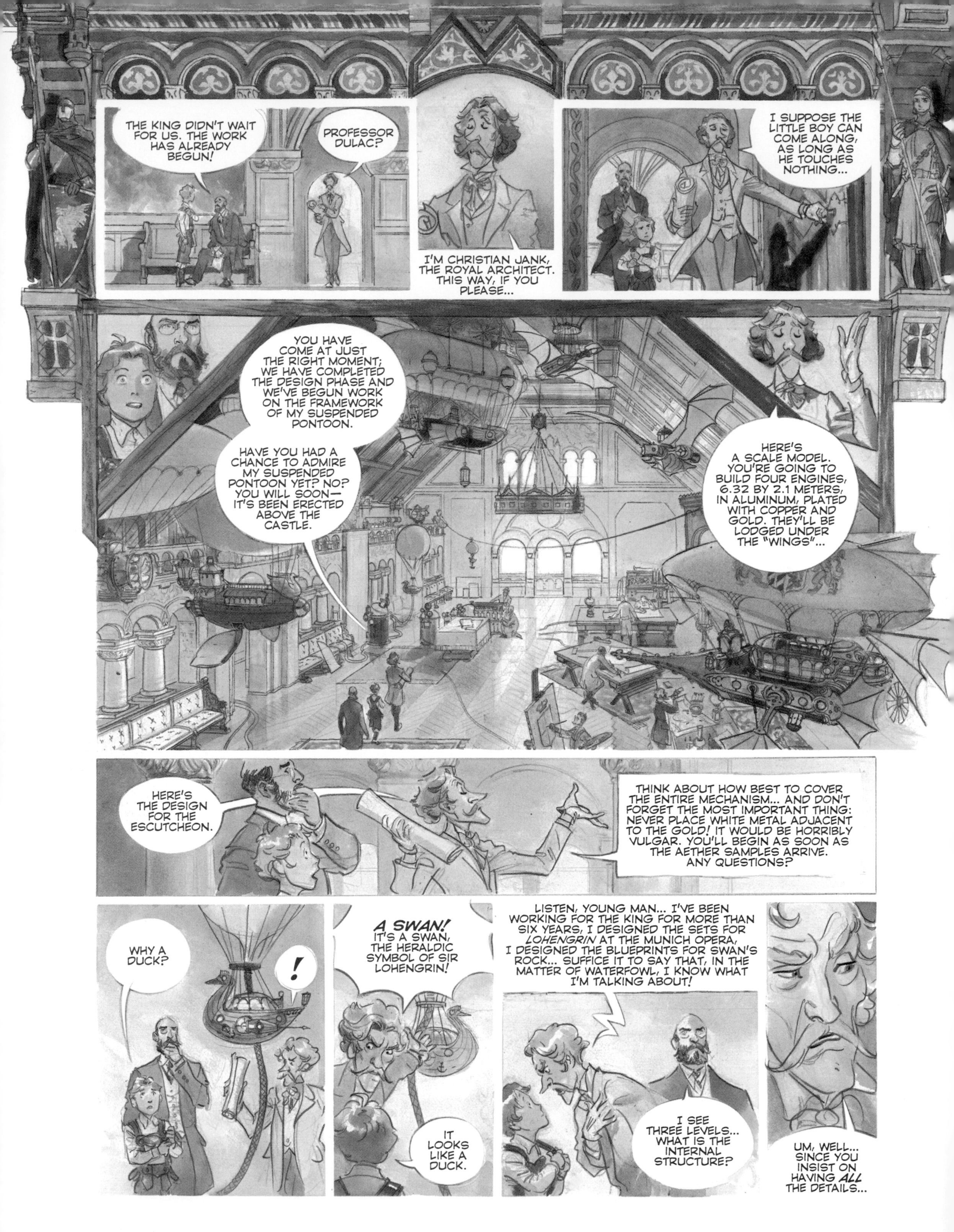
THE KING DIDN'T WAIT FOR US. THE WORK HAS ALREADY BEGUN!
PROFESSOR DULAC?
I'M CHRISTIAN JANK, THE ROYAL ARCHITECT. THIS WAY, IF YOU PLEASE...
I SUPPOSE THE LITTLE BOY CAN COME ALONG, AS LONG AS HE TOUCHES NOTHING...
YOU HAVE COME AT JUST THE RIGHT MOMENT; WE HAVE COMPLETED THE DESIGN PHASE AND WE'VE BEGUN WORK ON THE FRAMEWORK OF MY SUSPENDED PONTOON.
HAVE YOU HAD A CHANCE TO ADMIRE MY SUSPENDED PONTOON YET? NO? YOU WILL SOON— IT'S BEEN ERECTED ABOVE THE CASTLE.
HERE'S A SCALE MODEL. YOU'RE GOING TO BUILD FOUR ENGINES, 6.32 BY 2.1 METERS, IN ALUMINUM, PLATED WITH COPPER AND GOLD. THEY'LL BE LODGED UNDER THE "WINGS"...
HERE'S THE DESIGN FOR THE ESCUTCHEON.
THINK ABOUT HOW BEST TO COVER THE ENTIRE MECHANISM... AND DON'T FORGET THE MOST IMPORTANT THING: NEVER PLACE WHITE METAL ADJACENT TO THE GOLD! IT WOULD BE HORRIBLY VULGAR. YOU'LL BEGIN AS SOON AS THE AETHER SAMPLES ARRIVE. ANY QUESTIONS?
WHY A DUCK?
!
A SWAN! IT'S A SWAN, THE HERALDIC SYMBOL OF SIR LOHENGRIN!
IT LOOKS LIKE A DUCK.
LISTEN, YOUNG MAN... I'VE BEEN WORKING FOR THE KING FOR MORE THAN SIX YEARS, I DESIGNED THE SETS FOR *LOHENGRIN* AT THE MUNICH OPERA, I DESIGNED THE BLUEPRINTS FOR SWAN'S ROCK... SUFFICE IT TO SAY THAT, IN THE MATTER OF WATERFOWL, I KNOW WHAT I'M TALKING ABOUT!
I SEE THREE LEVELS... WHAT IS THE INTERNAL STRUCTURE?
UM, WELL... SINCE YOU INSIST ON HAVING *ALL* THE DETAILS...

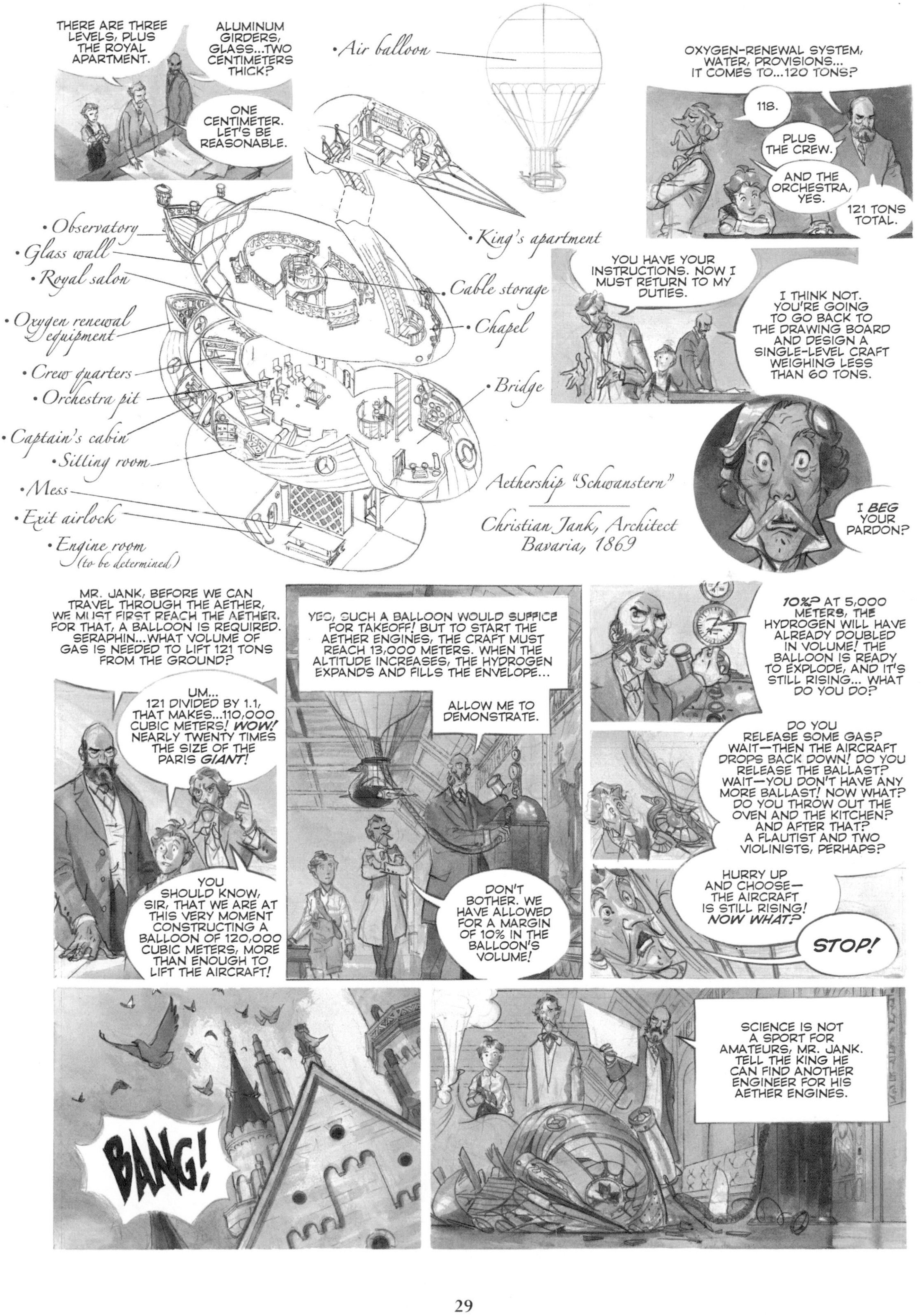
THERE ARE THREE LEVELS, PLUS THE ROYAL APARTMENT.
ALUMINUM GIRDERS, GLASS...TWO CENTIMETERS THICK?
ONE CENTIMETER. LET'S BE REASONABLE.
•Air balloon
•Observatory
•Glass wall
•Royal salon
•Oxygen renewal equipment
•Crew quarters
•Orchestra pit
•Captain's cabin
•Sitting room
•Mess
•Exit airlock
•Engine room (to be determined)
•King's apartment
•Cable storage
•Chapel
•Bridge
Aethership "Schwanstern"
Christian Jank, Architect
Bavaria, 1869
OXYGEN-RENEWAL SYSTEM, WATER, PROVISIONS... IT COMES TO...120 TONS?
118.
PLUS THE CREW.
AND THE ORCHESTRA, YES.
121 TONS TOTAL.
YOU HAVE YOUR INSTRUCTIONS. NOW I MUST RETURN TO MY DUTIES.
I THINK NOT. YOU'RE GOING TO GO BACK TO THE DRAWING BOARD AND DESIGN A SINGLE-LEVEL CRAFT WEIGHING LESS THAN 60 TONS.
I BEG YOUR PARDON?
MR. JANK, BEFORE WE CAN TRAVEL THROUGH THE AETHER, WE MUST FIRST REACH THE AETHER. FOR THAT, A BALLOON IS REQUIRED. SERAPHIN...WHAT VOLUME OF GAS IS NEEDED TO LIFT 121 TONS FROM THE GROUND?
UM... 121 DIVIDED BY 1.1, THAT MAKES...110,000 CUBIC METERS! WOW! NEARLY TWENTY TIMES THE SIZE OF THE PARIS GIANT!
YOU SIR, SHOULD KNOW, SIR, THAT WE ARE AT THIS VERY MOMENT CONSTRUCTING A BALLOON OF 120,000 CUBIC METERS, MORE THAN ENOUGH TO LIFT THE AIRCRAFT!
YES, SUCH A BALLOON WOULD SUFFICE FOR TAKEOFF! BUT TO START THE AETHER ENGINES, THE CRAFT MUST REACH 13,000 METERS. WHEN THE ALTITUDE INCREASES, THE HYDROGEN EXPANDS AND FILLS THE ENVELOPE...
ALLOW ME TO DEMONSTRATE.
DON'T BOTHER. WE HAVE ALLOWED FOR A MARGIN OF 10% IN THE BALLOON'S VOLUME!
10%? AT 5,000 METERS, THE HYDROGEN WILL HAVE ALREADY DOUBLED IN VOLUME! THE BALLOON IS READY TO EXPLODE, AND IT'S STILL RISING... WHAT DO YOU DO?
DO YOU RELEASE SOME GAS? WAIT—THEN THE AIRCRAFT DROPS BACK DOWN! DO YOU RELEASE THE BALLAST? WAIT—YOU DON'T HAVE ANY MORE BALLAST! NOW WHAT? DO YOU THROW OUT THE OVEN AND THE KITCHEN? AND AFTER THAT? A FLAUTIST AND TWO VIOLINISTS, PERHAPS?
HURRY UP AND CHOOSE—THE AIRCRAFT IS STILL RISING! NOW WHAT?
STOP!
BANG!
SCIENCE IS NOT A SPORT FOR AMATEURS, MR. JANK. TELL THE KING HE CAN FIND ANOTHER ENGINEER FOR HIS AETHER ENGINES.

HA HA HA! HAVE YOU SEEN YOURSELF IN A MIRROR?

?

HANS!

I CAN'T BELIEVE YOU WENT OUT DRESSED THAT WAY! **HA HA HA!**

THE SOCK, MY FRIEND! THE BAVARIAN SOCK IS ALWAYS WORN *ABOVE* THE ANKLE!!

OTHERWISE, IT LOOKS RIDICULOUS!

...

PROFESSOR, LOOK... FOUR HANDSOME AETHER RESERVOIRS, ALL AT YOUR DISPOSAL!

HAVE YOU SEEN THE MODELS IN THE MUSIC SALON? I'M THE ONE WHO MADE THEM!

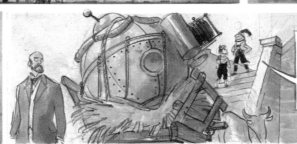

BY THE WAY, HAVE YOU SPOKEN WITH THE ARCHITECT?

NOT A CONGENIAL FELLOW, IS HE? COULD YOU HAVE A WORD WITH HIM ABOUT THE GAS DILATION AT ALTITUDE? HE NEVER LISTENS TO ANYTHING I SAY!

AHEM...

PROFESSOR?

I'VE BEEN THINKING— THE CRAFT MIGHT BE MORE ELEGANT IF WE REDUCE THE ORCHESTRA PIT. BUT I WILL NOT GO ANY FURTHER!

LET ME SEE THAT...

WHAT ARE YOU DOING WITH THAT PENCIL?

WELL, YES, PERHAPS THE ANTECHAMBER CAN BE REDUCED...

OR ELIMINATED

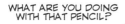

AS WELL AS THE SITTING ROOM...

IN THE NAME OF HEAVEN, PROFESSOR! YOU'RE NOT GOING TO REMOVE THE CHAPEL!

HANS, SERAPHIN, TAKE THE AETHER TO THE SUSPENDED PONTOON. I WILL SET UP MY LABORATORY THERE!

BUT...UM... THERE'S ALREADY AN ADEQUATE LABORATORY... UM...IN THE CELLAR!

THE ENGINES ARE THE HEART OF THE STRUCTURE. I WANT TO ASSEMBLE THEM ON THE LAUNCH PLATFORM.

I CAN'T BELIEVE IT! YOUR FATHER PUT OLD JANK IN HIS PLACE!

LET'S GO!

I'M COMING! WHERE IS THIS SUSPENDED PONTOON?

30

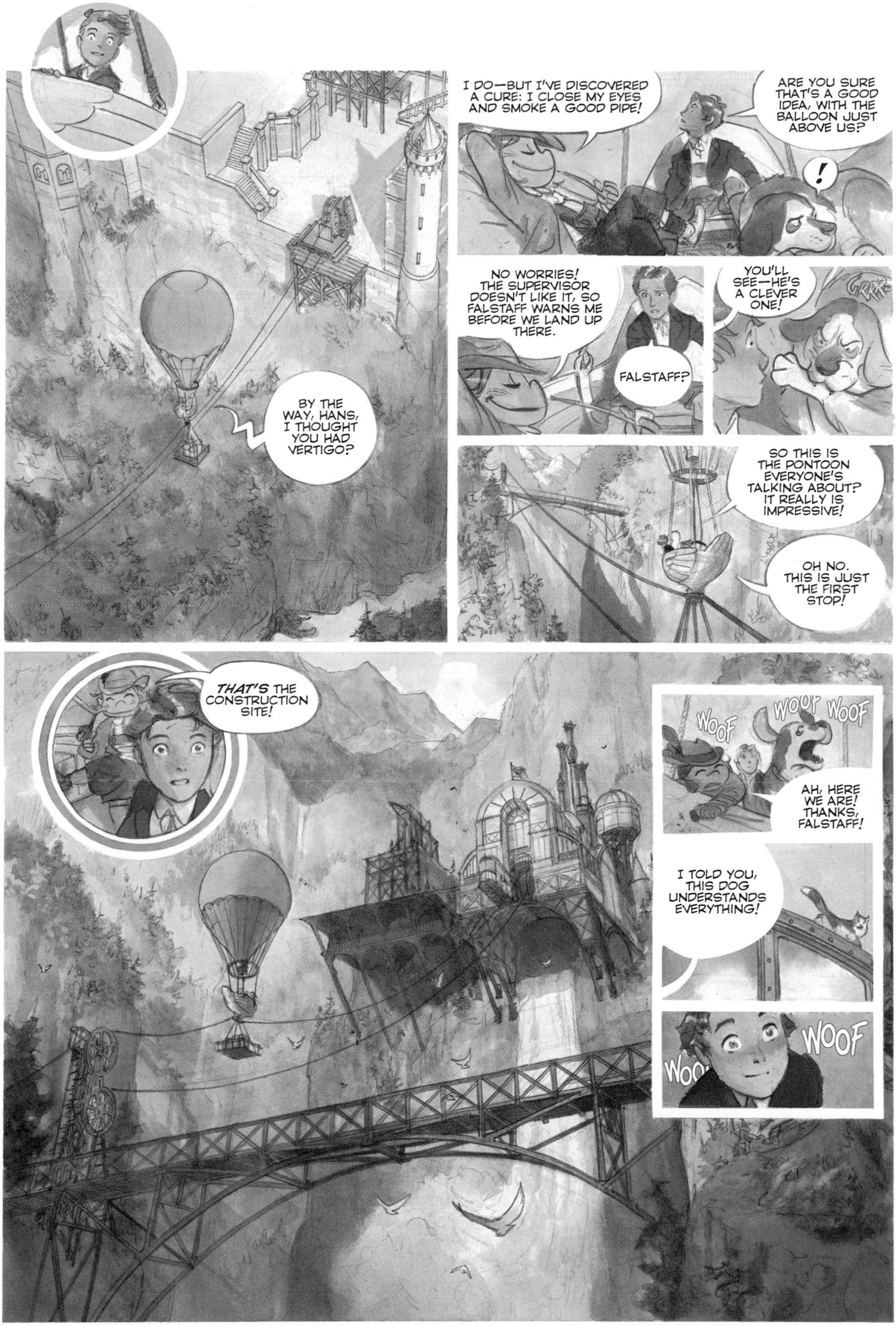

BY THE WAY, HANS, I THOUGHT YOU HAD VERTIGO?
I DO—BUT I'VE DISCOVERED A CURE: I CLOSE MY EYES AND SMOKE A GOOD PIPE!
ARE YOU SURE THAT'S A GOOD IDEA, WITH THE BALLOON JUST ABOVE US?
!
NO WORRIES! THE SUPERVISOR DOESN'T LIKE IT, SO FALSTAFF WARNS ME BEFORE WE LAND UP THERE.
FALSTAFF?
YOU'LL SEE—HE'S A CLEVER ONE!
GRRR
SO THIS IS THE PONTOON EVERYONE'S TALKING ABOUT? IT REALLY IS IMPRESSIVE!
OH NO. THIS IS JUST THE FIRST STOP!
THAT'S THE CONSTRUCTION SITE!
WOOF WOOF WOOF
AH, HERE WE ARE! THANKS, FALSTAFF!
I TOLD YOU, THIS DOG UNDERSTANDS EVERYTHING!
WOOF WOOF

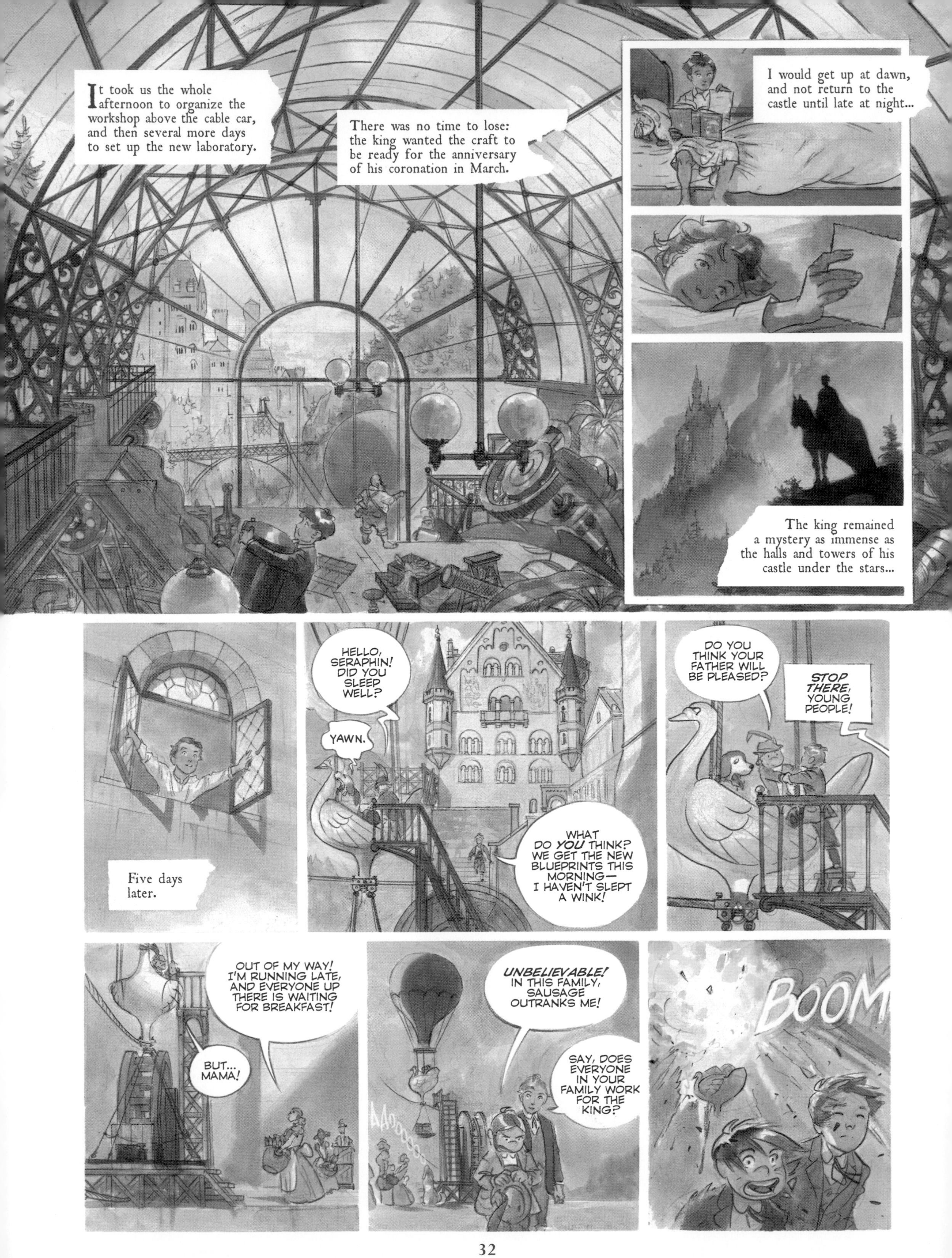
It took us the whole afternoon to organize the workshop above the cable car, and then several more days to set up the new laboratory.
There was no time to lose: the king wanted the craft to be ready for the anniversary of his coronation in March.
I would get up at dawn, and not return to the castle until late at night...
The king remained a mystery as immense as the halls and towers of his castle under the stars...
Five days later.
HELLO, SERAPHIN! DID YOU SLEEP WELL?
YAWN.
WHAT DO YOU THINK? WE GET THE NEW BLUEPRINTS THIS MORNING— I HAVEN'T SLEPT A WINK!
DO YOU THINK YOUR FATHER WILL BE PLEASED?
STOP THERE, YOUNG PEOPLE!
OUT OF MY WAY! I'M RUNNING LATE, AND EVERYONE UP THERE IS WAITING FOR BREAKFAST!
BUT... MAMA!
UNBELIEVABLE! IN THIS FAMILY, SAUSAGE OUTRANKS ME!
SAY, DOES EVERYONE IN YOUR FAMILY WORK FOR THE KING?
BOOM

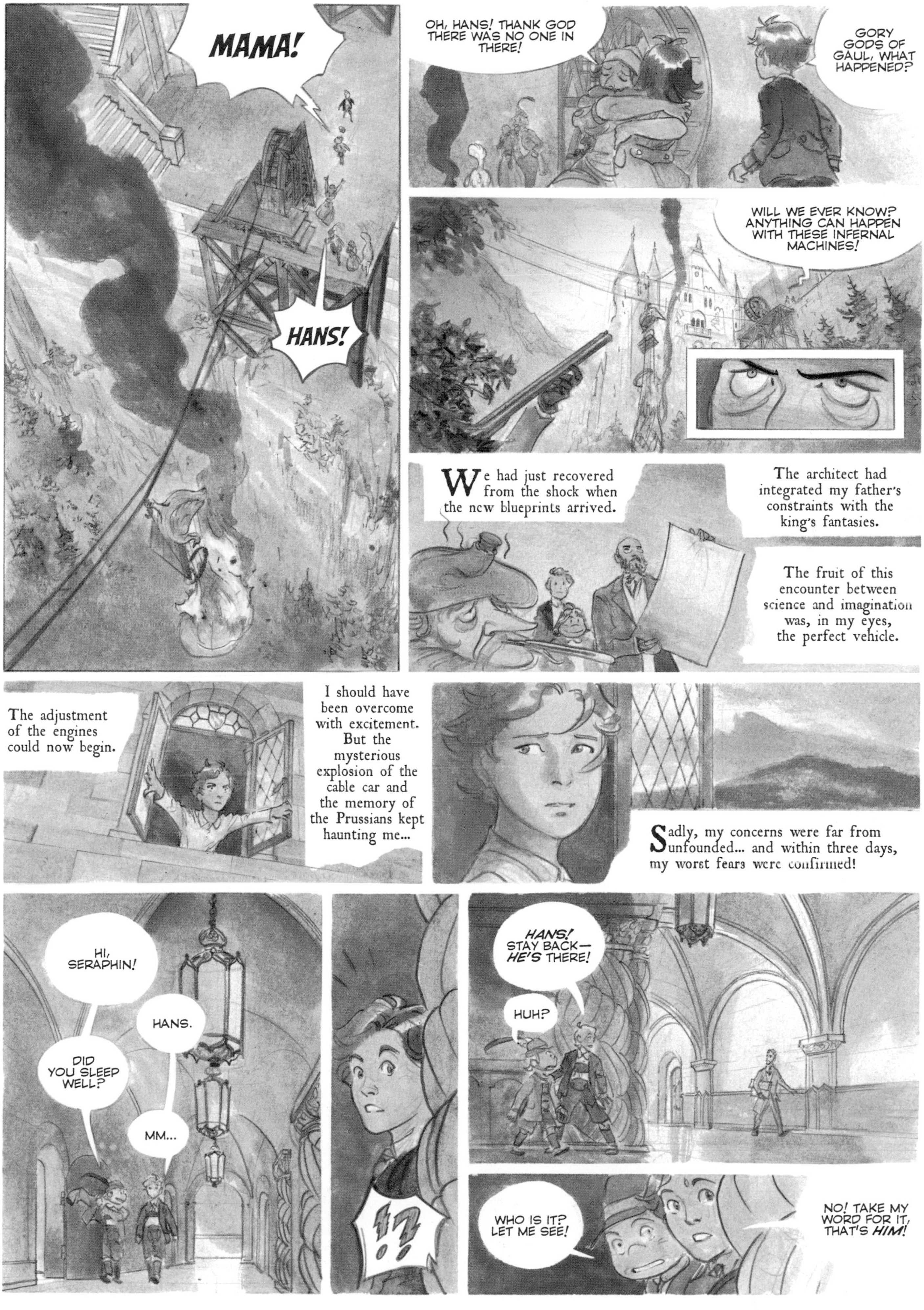
MAMA!
HANS!
OH, HANS! THANK GOD THERE WAS NO ONE IN THERE!
GORY GODS OF GAUL, WHAT HAPPENED?
WILL WE EVER KNOW? ANYTHING CAN HAPPEN WITH THESE INFERNAL MACHINES!
We had just recovered from the shock when the new blueprints arrived.
The architect had integrated my father's constraints with the king's fantasies.
The fruit of this encounter between science and imagination was, in my eyes, the perfect vehicle.
The adjustment of the engines could now begin.
I should have been overcome with excitement. But the mysterious explosion of the cable car and the memory of the Prussians kept haunting me...
Sadly, my concerns were far from unfounded... and within three days, my worst fears were confirmed!
HI, SERAPHIN!
HANS.
DID YOU SLEEP WELL?
MM...
!?
HANS! STAY BACK— HE'S THERE!
HUH?
WHO IS IT? LET ME SEE!
NO! TAKE MY WORD FOR IT, THAT'S HIM!

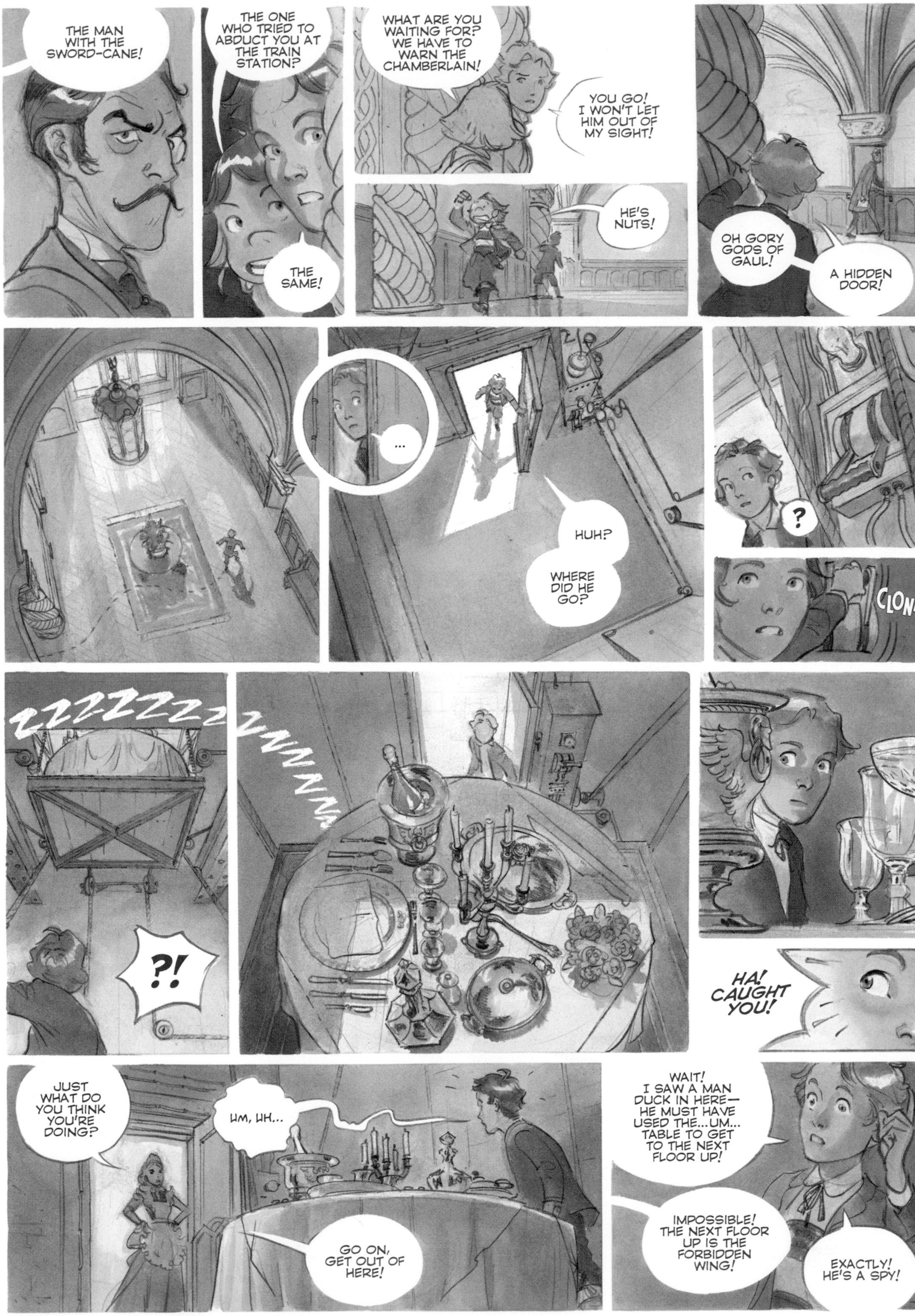
THE MAN WITH THE SWORD-CANE!
THE ONE WHO TRIED TO ABDUCT YOU AT THE TRAIN STATION?
THE SAME!
WHAT ARE YOU WAITING FOR? WE HAVE TO WARN THE CHAMBERLAIN!
YOU GO! I WON'T LET HIM OUT OF MY SIGHT!
HE'S NUTS!
OH GORY GODS OF GAUL!
A HIDDEN DOOR!
...
HUH?
WHERE DID HE GO?
?
CLONK
ZZZZZZZZZZZNNNNNN
?!
HA! CAUGHT YOU!
JUST WHAT DO YOU THINK YOU'RE DOING?
UM, UH...
GO ON, GET OUT OF HERE!
WAIT! I SAW A MAN DUCK IN HERE—HE MUST HAVE USED THE...UM... TABLE TO GET TO THE NEXT FLOOR UP!
IMPOSSIBLE! THE NEXT FLOOR UP IS THE FORBIDDEN WING!
EXACTLY! HE'S A SPY!

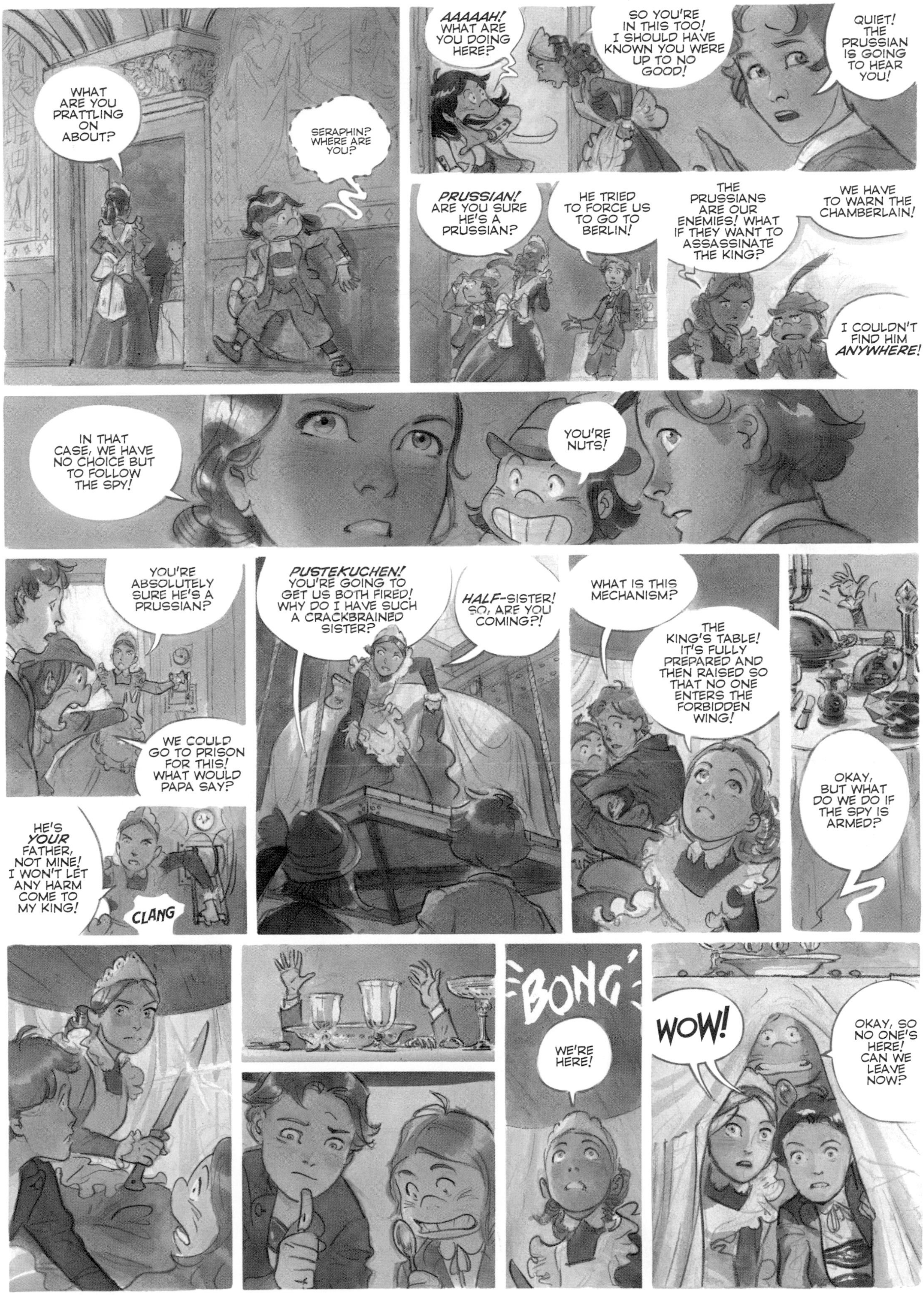
WHAT ARE YOU PRATTLING ON ABOUT?
SERAPHIN? WHERE ARE YOU?
AAAAAH! WHAT ARE YOU DOING HERE?
SO YOU'RE IN THIS TOO! I SHOULD HAVE KNOWN YOU WERE UP TO NO GOOD!
QUIET! THE PRUSSIAN IS GOING TO HEAR YOU!
PRUSSIAN! ARE YOU SURE HE'S A PRUSSIAN?
HE TRIED TO FORCE US TO GO TO BERLIN!
THE PRUSSIANS ARE OUR ENEMIES! WHAT IF THEY WANT TO ASSASSINATE THE KING?
WE HAVE TO WARN THE CHAMBERLAIN!
I COULDN'T FIND HIM ANYWHERE!
IN THAT CASE, WE HAVE NO CHOICE BUT TO FOLLOW THE SPY!
YOU'RE NUTS!
YOU'RE ABSOLUTELY SURE HE'S A PRUSSIAN?
WE COULD GO TO PRISON FOR THIS! WHAT WOULD PAPA SAY?
HE'S YOUR FATHER, NOT MINE! I WON'T LET ANY HARM COME TO MY KING!
CLANG
PUSTEKUCHEN! YOU'RE GOING TO GET US BOTH FIRED! WHY DO I HAVE SUCH A CRACKBRAINED SISTER?
HALF-SISTER! SO, ARE YOU COMING?!
WHAT IS THIS MECHANISM?
THE KING'S TABLE! IT'S FULLY PREPARED AND THEN RAISED SO THAT NO ONE ENTERS THE FORBIDDEN WING!
OKAY, BUT WHAT DO WE DO IF THE SPY IS ARMED?
BONG
WE'RE HERE!
WOW!
OKAY, SO NO ONE'S HERE! CAN WE LEAVE NOW?

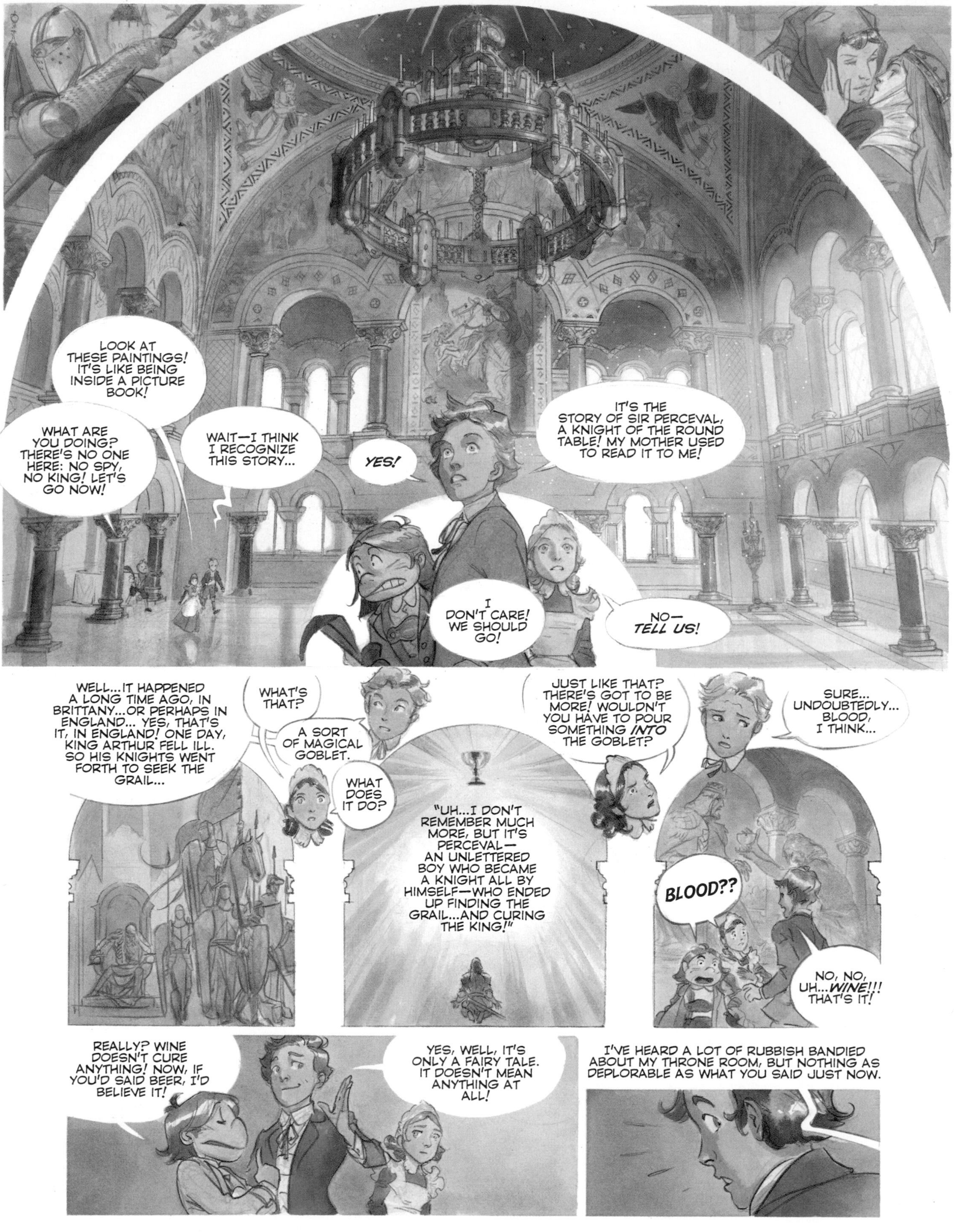

LOOK AT THESE PAINTINGS! IT'S LIKE BEING INSIDE A PICTURE BOOK!
WHAT ARE YOU DOING? THERE'S NO ONE HERE: NO SPY, NO KING! LET'S GO NOW!
WAIT—I THINK I RECOGNIZE THIS STORY...
YES!
IT'S THE STORY OF SIR PERCEVAL, A KNIGHT OF THE ROUND TABLE! MY MOTHER USED TO READ IT TO ME!
I DON'T CARE! WE SHOULD GO!
NO—TELL US!
WELL...IT HAPPENED A LONG TIME AGO, IN BRITTANY...OR PERHAPS IN ENGLAND... YES, THAT'S IT, IN ENGLAND! ONE DAY, KING ARTHUR FELL ILL. SO HIS KNIGHTS WENT FORTH TO SEEK THE GRAIL...
WHAT'S THAT?
A SORT OF MAGICAL GOBLET.
WHAT DOES IT DO?
"UH...I DON'T REMEMBER MUCH MORE, BUT IT'S PERCEVAL—AN UNLETTERED BOY WHO BECAME A KNIGHT ALL BY HIMSELF—WHO ENDED UP FINDING THE GRAIL...AND CURING THE KING!"
JUST LIKE THAT? THERE'S GOT TO BE MORE! WOULDN'T YOU HAVE TO POUR SOMETHING INTO THE GOBLET?
SURE... UNDOUBTEDLY... BLOOD, I THINK...
BLOOD??
NO, NO, UH...WINE!!! THAT'S IT!
REALLY? WINE DOESN'T CURE ANYTHING! NOW, IF YOU'D SAID BEER, I'D BELIEVE IT!
YES, WELL, IT'S ONLY A FAIRY TALE. IT DOESN'T MEAN ANYTHING AT ALL!
I'VE HEARD A LOT OF RUBBISH BANDIED ABOUT MY THRONE ROOM, BUT NOTHING AS DEPLORABLE AS WHAT YOU SAID JUST NOW.

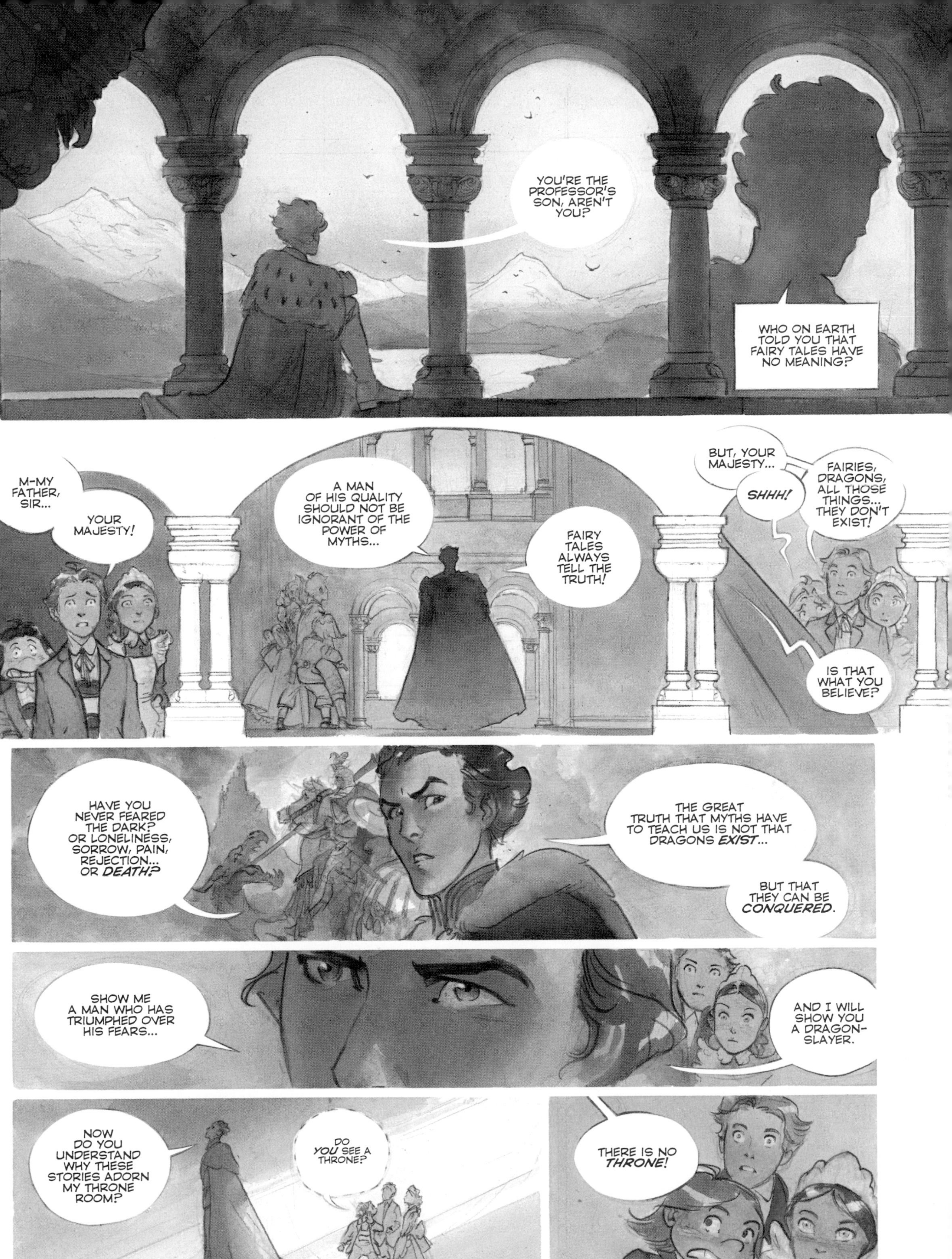
YOU'RE THE PROFESSOR'S SON, AREN'T YOU?
WHO ON EARTH TOLD YOU THAT FAIRY TALES HAVE NO MEANING?
M-MY FATHER, SIR...
YOUR MAJESTY!
A MAN OF HIS QUALITY SHOULD NOT BE IGNORANT OF THE POWER OF MYTHS...
FAIRY TALES ALWAYS TELL THE TRUTH!
BUT, YOUR MAJESTY...
SHHH!
FAIRIES, DRAGONS, ALL THOSE THINGS... THEY DON'T EXIST!
IS THAT WHAT YOU BELIEVE?
HAVE YOU NEVER FEARED THE DARK? OR LONELINESS, SORROW, PAIN, REJECTION... OR DEATH?
THE GREAT TRUTH THAT MYTHS HAVE TO TEACH US IS NOT THAT DRAGONS EXIST...
BUT THAT THEY CAN BE CONQUERED.
SHOW ME A MAN WHO HAS TRIUMPHED OVER HIS FEARS...
AND I WILL SHOW YOU A DRAGON-SLAYER.
NOW DO YOU UNDERSTAND WHY THESE STORIES ADORN MY THRONE ROOM?
DO YOU SEE A THRONE?
THERE IS NO THRONE!

AT THE MOMENT...

I AM WAITING FOR YOU TO EXPLAIN WHY YOU CHOSE TO VIOLATE THE MOST SACRED RULE OF THIS CASTLE!

UH, WELL, UM...

IT ALL BEGAN AT THE LILLE TRAIN STATION...

THERE'S A PRUSSIAN SPY IN THE HEART OF THE CASTLE!

WHAT?

YOUR MAJESTY!

YOUR MAJESTY, PARDON ME FOR FAILING TO PREVENT THE INTRUSION OF THESE WRETCHES!

AHA!

IT'S *HIM*!

YOUR MAJESTY! YOU MUST BELIEVE ME...

SERAPHIN!

THIS MAN TRIED TO ABDUCT US AND TAKE US TO BERLIN! CALL THE GUARD! CALL THE CHAMBERLAIN!

SERAPHIN, *STOP*!...

HE *IS* THE CHAMBERLAIN!

YOUR MAJESTY, LET ME HANDLE THIS MATTER. THESE NOSY YOUNGSTERS WILL BE DULY PUNISHED!

...

NO...NO! I'M *POSITIVE*! *YOU* CAUSED THE CABLE CAR EXPLOSION! YOU KNEW THAT I WOULD RECOGNIZE YOU, AND SO YOU LURED ME HERE INTO THIS TRAP! NOW NO ONE WILL BELIEVE ME!

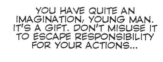

YOU HAVE QUITE AN IMAGINATION, YOUNG MAN. IT'S A GIFT. DON'T MISUSE IT TO ESCAPE RESPONSIBILITY FOR YOUR ACTIONS...

DON'T WORRY, YOUR MAJESTY... I'LL MAKE AN EXAMPLE OF THEM THAT BAVARIA WILL NOT SOON FORGET!

NO, VON GUDDEN... DON'T BE TOO HARSH...

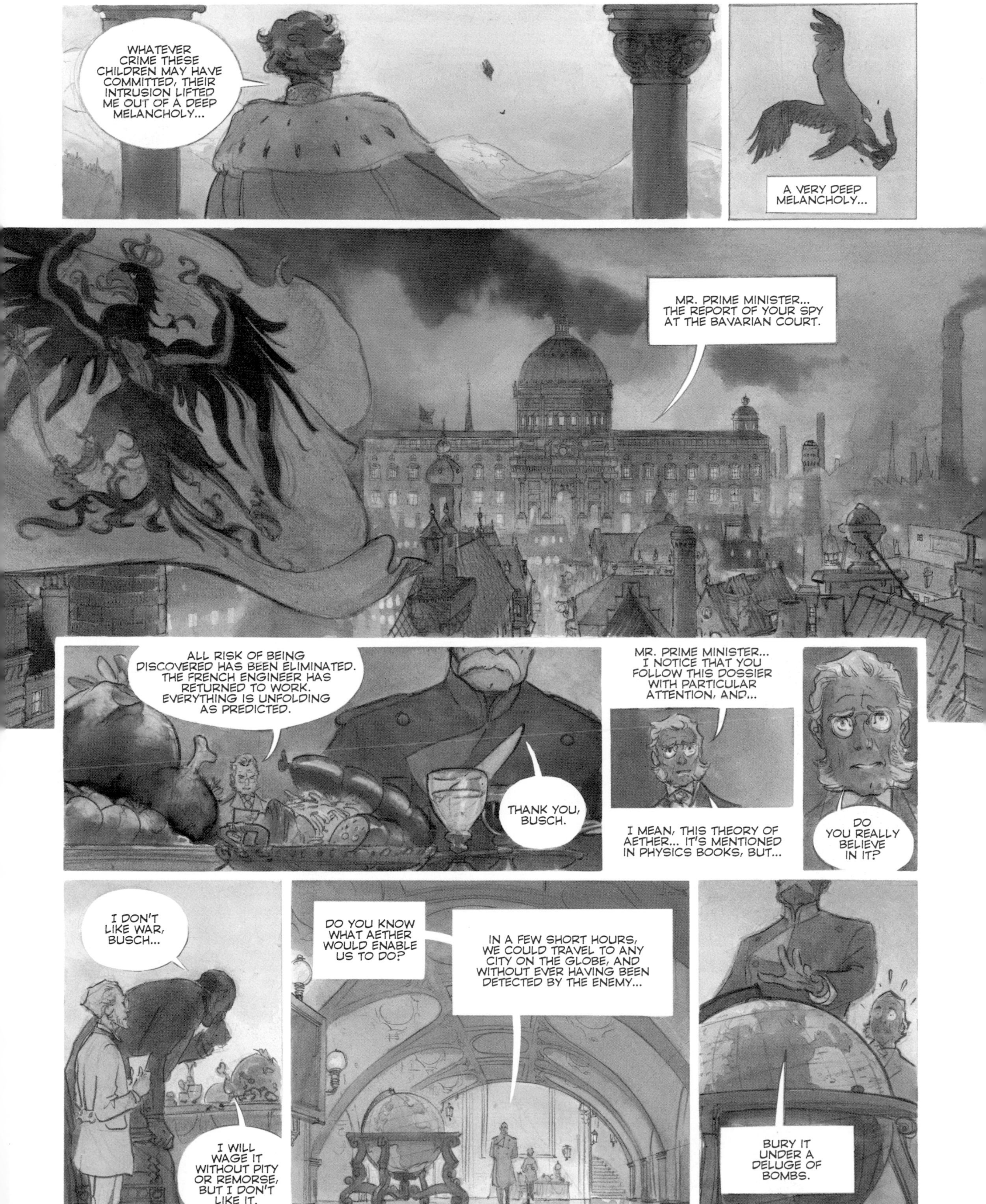
WHATEVER CRIME THESE CHILDREN MAY HAVE COMMITTED, THEIR INTRUSION LIFTED ME OUT OF A DEEP MELANCHOLY...
A VERY DEEP MELANCHOLY...
MR. PRIME MINISTER... THE REPORT OF YOUR SPY AT THE BAVARIAN COURT.
ALL RISK OF BEING DISCOVERED HAS BEEN ELIMINATED. THE FRENCH ENGINEER HAS RETURNED TO WORK. EVERYTHING IS UNFOLDING AS PREDICTED.
THANK YOU, BUSCH.
MR. PRIME MINISTER... I NOTICE THAT YOU FOLLOW THIS DOSSIER WITH PARTICULAR ATTENTION, AND...
I MEAN, THIS THEORY OF AETHER... IT'S MENTIONED IN PHYSICS BOOKS, BUT...
DO YOU REALLY BELIEVE IN IT?
I DON'T LIKE WAR, BUSCH...
I WILL WAGE IT WITHOUT PITY OR REMORSE, BUT I DON'T LIKE IT.
DO YOU KNOW WHAT AETHER WOULD ENABLE US TO DO?
IN A FEW SHORT HOURS, WE COULD TRAVEL TO ANY CITY ON THE GLOBE, AND WITHOUT EVER HAVING BEEN DETECTED BY THE ENEMY...
BURY IT UNDER A DELUGE OF BOMBS.

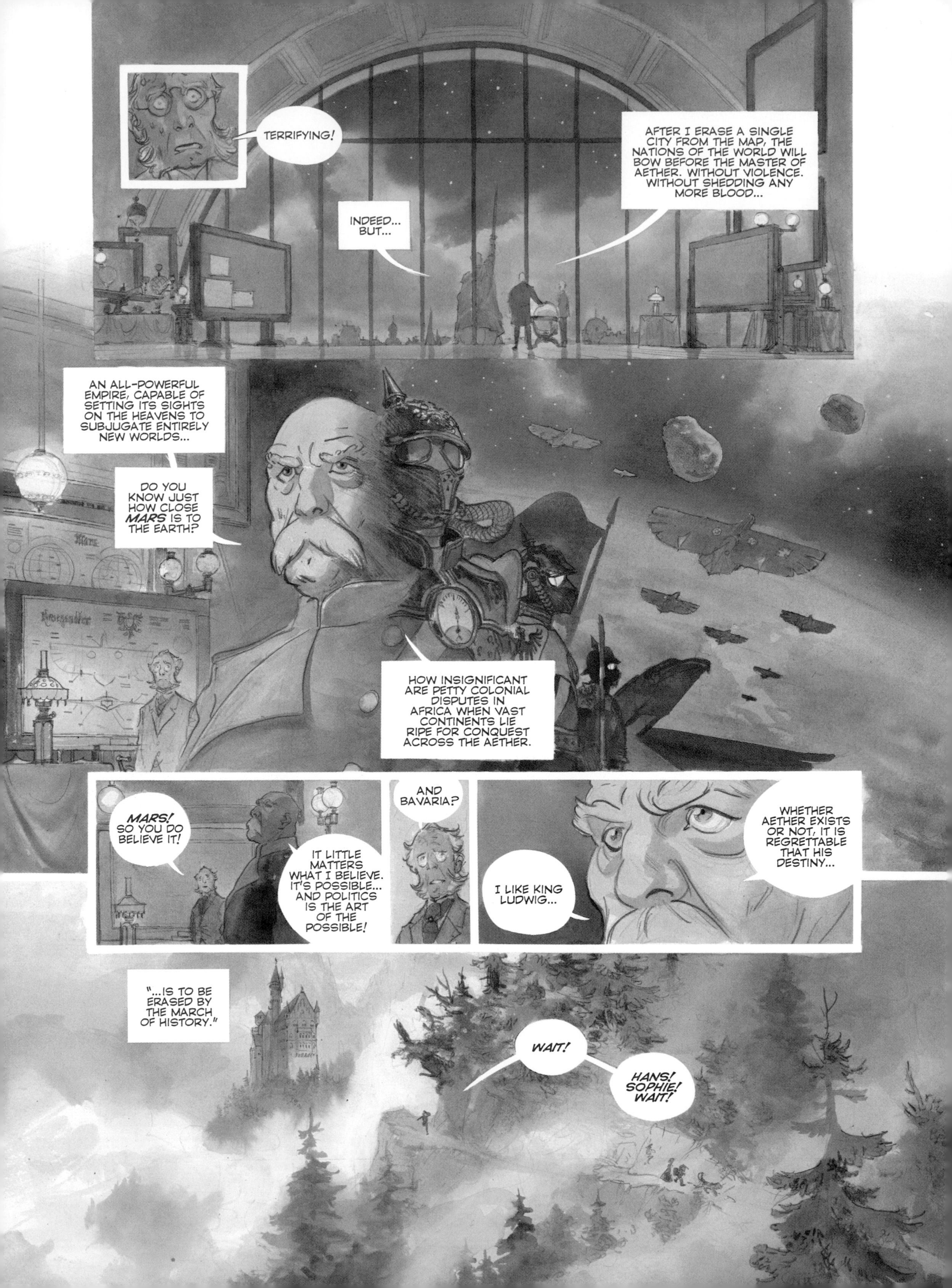
TERRIFYING!
AFTER I ERASE A SINGLE CITY FROM THE MAP, THE NATIONS OF THE WORLD WILL BOW BEFORE THE MASTER OF AETHER. WITHOUT VIOLENCE. WITHOUT SHEDDING ANY MORE BLOOD...
INDEED... BUT...
AN ALL-POWERFUL EMPIRE, CAPABLE OF SETTING ITS SIGHTS ON THE HEAVENS TO SUBJUGATE ENTIRELY NEW WORLDS...
DO YOU KNOW JUST HOW CLOSE MARS IS TO THE EARTH?
HOW INSIGNIFICANT ARE PETTY COLONIAL DISPUTES IN AFRICA WHEN VAST CONTINENTS LIE RIPE FOR CONQUEST ACROSS THE AETHER.
MARS! SO YOU DO BELIEVE IT!
IT LITTLE MATTERS WHAT I BELIEVE. IT'S POSSIBLE... AND POLITICS IS THE ART OF THE POSSIBLE!
AND BAVARIA?
I LIKE KING LUDWIG...
WHETHER AETHER EXISTS OR NOT, IT IS REGRETTABLE THAT HIS DESTINY...
"...IS TO BE ERASED BY THE MARCH OF HISTORY."
WAIT!
HANS! SOPHIE! WAIT!

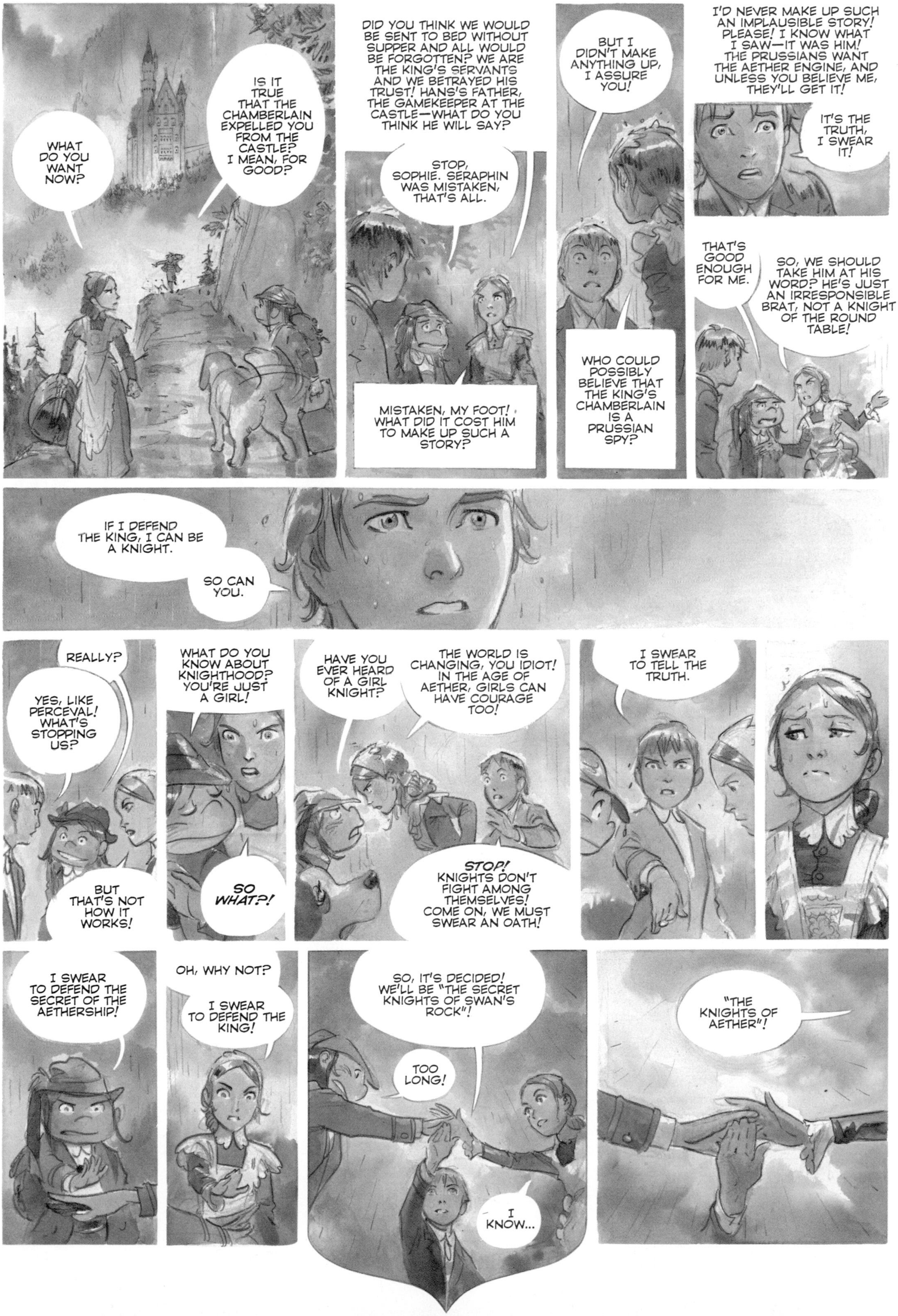
WHAT DO YOU WANT NOW?
IS IT TRUE THAT THE CHAMBERLAIN EXPELLED YOU FROM THE CASTLE? I MEAN, FOR GOOD?
DID YOU THINK WE WOULD BE SENT TO BED WITHOUT SUPPER AND ALL WOULD BE FORGOTTEN? WE ARE THE KING'S SERVANTS AND WE BETRAYED HIS TRUST! HANS'S FATHER, THE GAMEKEEPER AT THE CASTLE—WHAT DO YOU THINK HE WILL SAY?
STOP, SOPHIE. SERAPHIN WAS MISTAKEN, THAT'S ALL.
MISTAKEN, MY FOOT! WHAT DID IT COST HIM TO MAKE UP SUCH A STORY?
BUT I DIDN'T MAKE ANYTHING UP, I ASSURE YOU!
WHO COULD POSSIBLY BELIEVE THAT THE KING'S CHAMBERLAIN IS A PRUSSIAN SPY?
I'D NEVER MAKE UP SUCH AN IMPLAUSIBLE STORY! PLEASE! I KNOW WHAT I SAW—IT WAS HIM! THE PRUSSIANS WANT THE AETHER ENGINE, AND UNLESS YOU BELIEVE ME, THEY'LL GET IT!
IT'S THE TRUTH, I SWEAR IT!
THAT'S GOOD ENOUGH FOR ME.
SO, WE SHOULD TAKE HIM AT HIS WORD? HE'S JUST AN IRRESPONSIBLE BRAT, NOT A KNIGHT OF THE ROUND TABLE!
IF I DEFEND THE KING, I CAN BE A KNIGHT.
SO CAN YOU.
REALLY?
YES, LIKE PERCEVAL! WHAT'S STOPPING US?
BUT THAT'S NOT HOW IT WORKS!
WHAT DO YOU KNOW ABOUT KNIGHTHOOD? YOU'RE JUST A GIRL!
SO WHAT?!
HAVE YOU EVER HEARD OF A GIRL KNIGHT?
THE WORLD IS CHANGING, YOU IDIOT! IN THE AGE OF AETHER, GIRLS CAN HAVE COURAGE TOO!
STOP! KNIGHTS DON'T FIGHT AMONG THEMSELVES! COME ON, WE MUST SWEAR AN OATH!
I SWEAR TO TELL THE TRUTH.
I SWEAR TO DEFEND THE SECRET OF THE AETHERSHIP!
OH, WHY NOT?
I SWEAR TO DEFEND THE KING!
SO, IT'S DECIDED! WE'LL BE "THE SECRET KNIGHTS OF SWAN'S ROCK"!
TOO LONG!
I KNOW...
"THE KNIGHTS OF AETHER"!

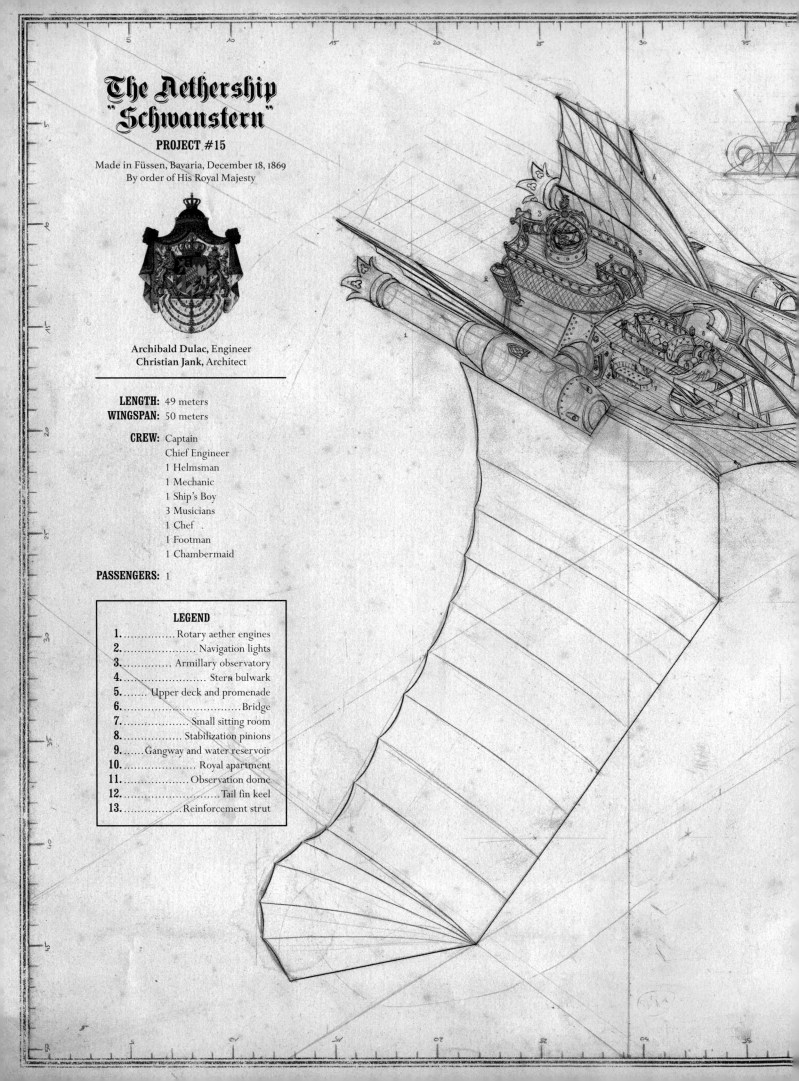

The Aethership "Schwanstern"

PROJECT #15

Made in Füssen, Bavaria, December 18, 1869
By order of His Royal Majesty

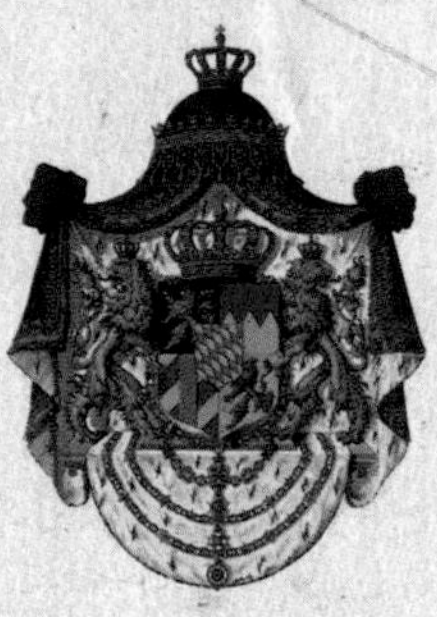

Archibald Dulac, Engineer
Christian Jank, Architect

LENGTH: 49 meters
WINGSPAN: 50 meters

CREW: Captain
Chief Engineer
1 Helmsman
1 Mechanic
1 Ship's Boy
3 Musicians
1 Chef
1 Footman
1 Chambermaid

PASSENGERS: 1

LEGEND

1. .... Rotary aether engines
2. .... Navigation lights
3. .... Armillary observatory
4. .... Stern bulwark
5. .... Upper deck and promenade
6. ....Bridge
7. .... Small sitting room
8. .... Stabilization pinions
9. ....Gangway and water reservoir
10. .... Royal apartment
11. .... Observation dome
12. ....Tail fin keel
13. ....Reinforcement strut

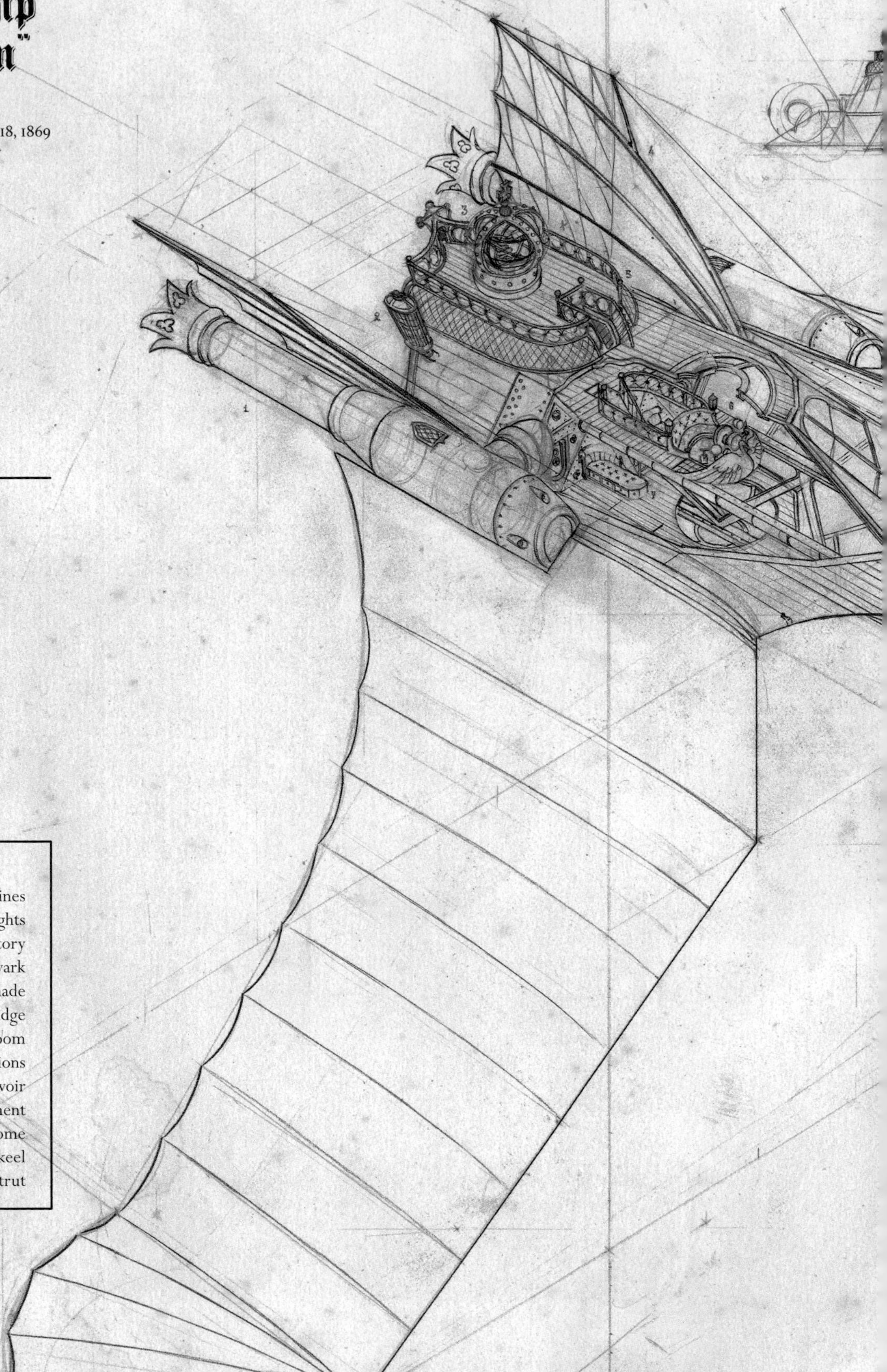

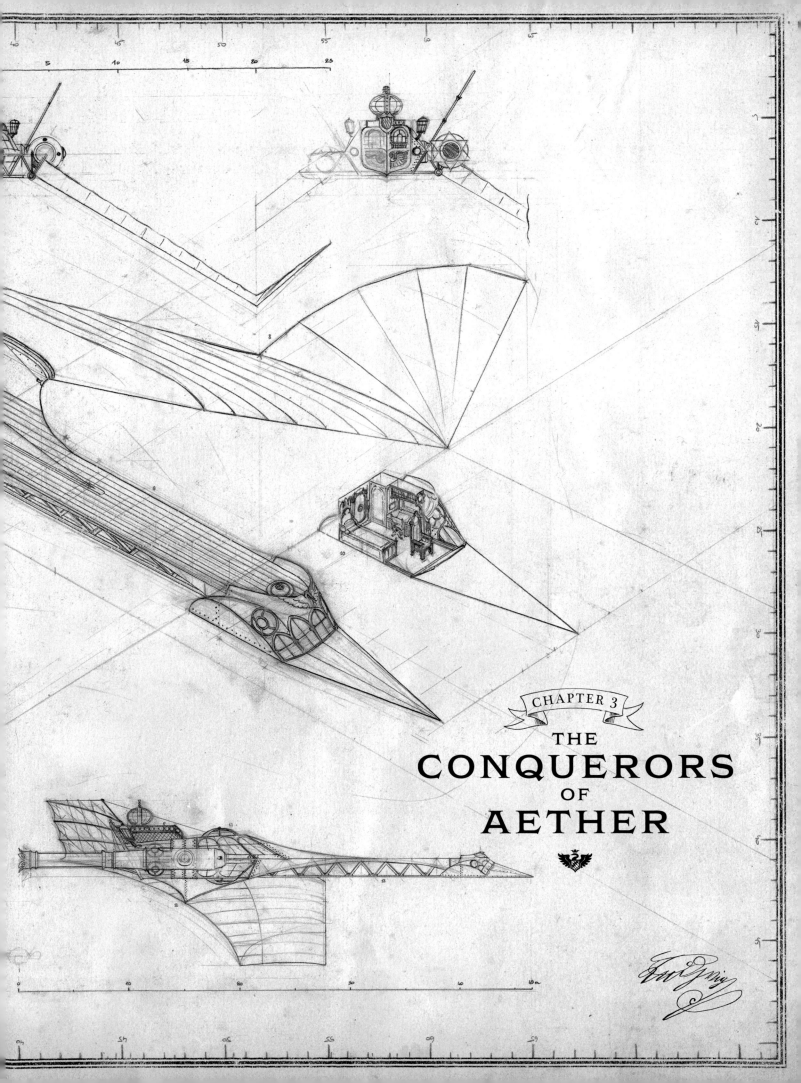

CHAPTER 3

THE
CONQUERORS
OF
AETHER

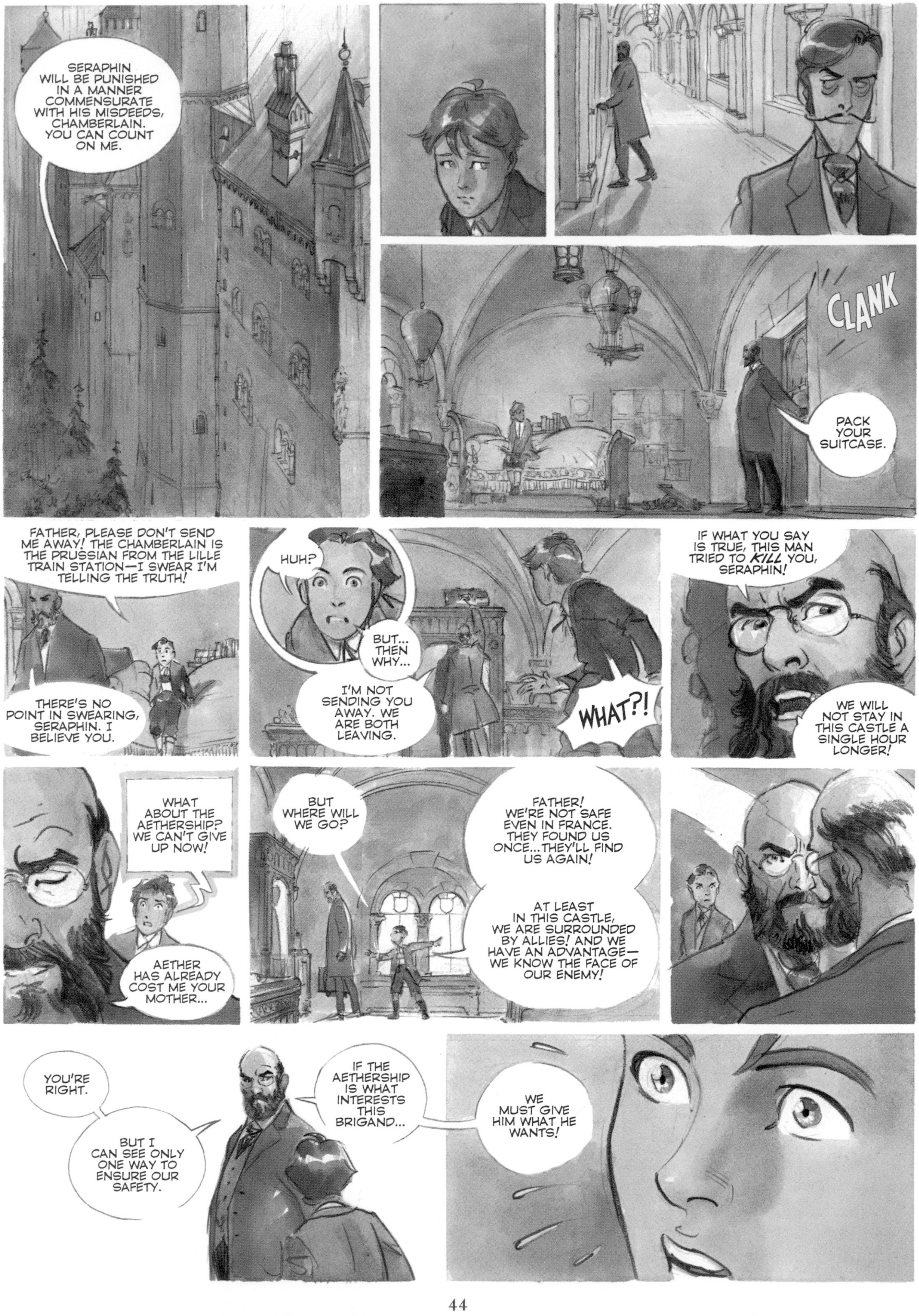
SERAPHIN WILL BE PUNISHED IN A MANNER COMMENSURATE WITH HIS MISDEEDS, CHAMBERLAIN. YOU CAN COUNT ON ME.
CLANK
PACK YOUR SUITCASE.
FATHER, PLEASE DON'T SEND ME AWAY! THE CHAMBERLAIN IS THE PRUSSIAN FROM THE LILLE TRAIN STATION—I SWEAR I'M TELLING THE TRUTH!
THERE'S NO POINT IN SWEARING, SERAPHIN. I BELIEVE YOU.
HUH?
BUT... THEN WHY...
I'M NOT SENDING YOU AWAY. WE ARE BOTH LEAVING.
WHAT?!
IF WHAT YOU SAY IS TRUE, THIS MAN TRIED TO KILL YOU, SERAPHIN!
WE WILL NOT STAY IN THIS CASTLE A SINGLE HOUR LONGER!
WHAT ABOUT THE AETHERSHIP? WE CAN'T GIVE UP NOW!
AETHER HAS ALREADY COST ME YOUR MOTHER...
BUT WHERE WILL WE GO?
FATHER! WE'RE NOT SAFE EVEN IN FRANCE. THEY FOUND US ONCE...THEY'LL FIND US AGAIN!
AT LEAST IN THIS CASTLE, WE ARE SURROUNDED BY ALLIES! AND WE HAVE AN ADVANTAGE—WE KNOW THE FACE OF OUR ENEMY!
YOU'RE RIGHT.
BUT I CAN SEE ONLY ONE WAY TO ENSURE OUR SAFETY.
IF THE AETHERSHIP IS WHAT INTERESTS THIS BRIGAND...
WE MUST GIVE HIM WHAT HE WANTS!

From that day on, while the framework of the aethership was taking shape on the pontoon, my father was developing its heart: the aether engines.

At the end of each day, he locked his notes in the strongbox furnished by the chamberlain...

ONE CAN NEVER BE TOO CAREFUL!

As for me, disgraced in everyone's eyes, I spent my days confined to quarters, doing homework.

Of course, every night the chamberlain would open the strongbox and faithfully copy all my father's notes.

Because all the notes were fake. In reality, my work each day consisted of copying over my father's notes into my mother's logbook...

It was my favorite moment of the day...

Next, I would modify the originals—changing numbers, altering diagrams, inventing formulas—to make them unusable...

It was a titanic effort, but I was amply rewarded by the knowledge that each evening the chamberlain would spend hours copying my nonsense!

As long as the chamberlain believed he was getting what he wanted, we were out of danger! Still, I had to endure my confinement within the castle... I worried about the other Knights of Aether...and hoped their parents had been merciful...

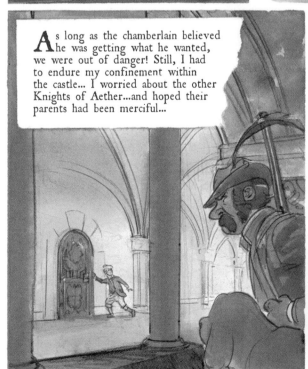

My first encounter with Hans's father was not at all encouraging.

Since the construction work was running late, my father found a replacement for Hans. A boy from a neighboring village, with good references... I was outraged that someone else was taking over my friend's job. Besides, he might also have been a spy...

In short, I gave him a glacial welcome.

SO, YOU'RE THE NEW BOY?

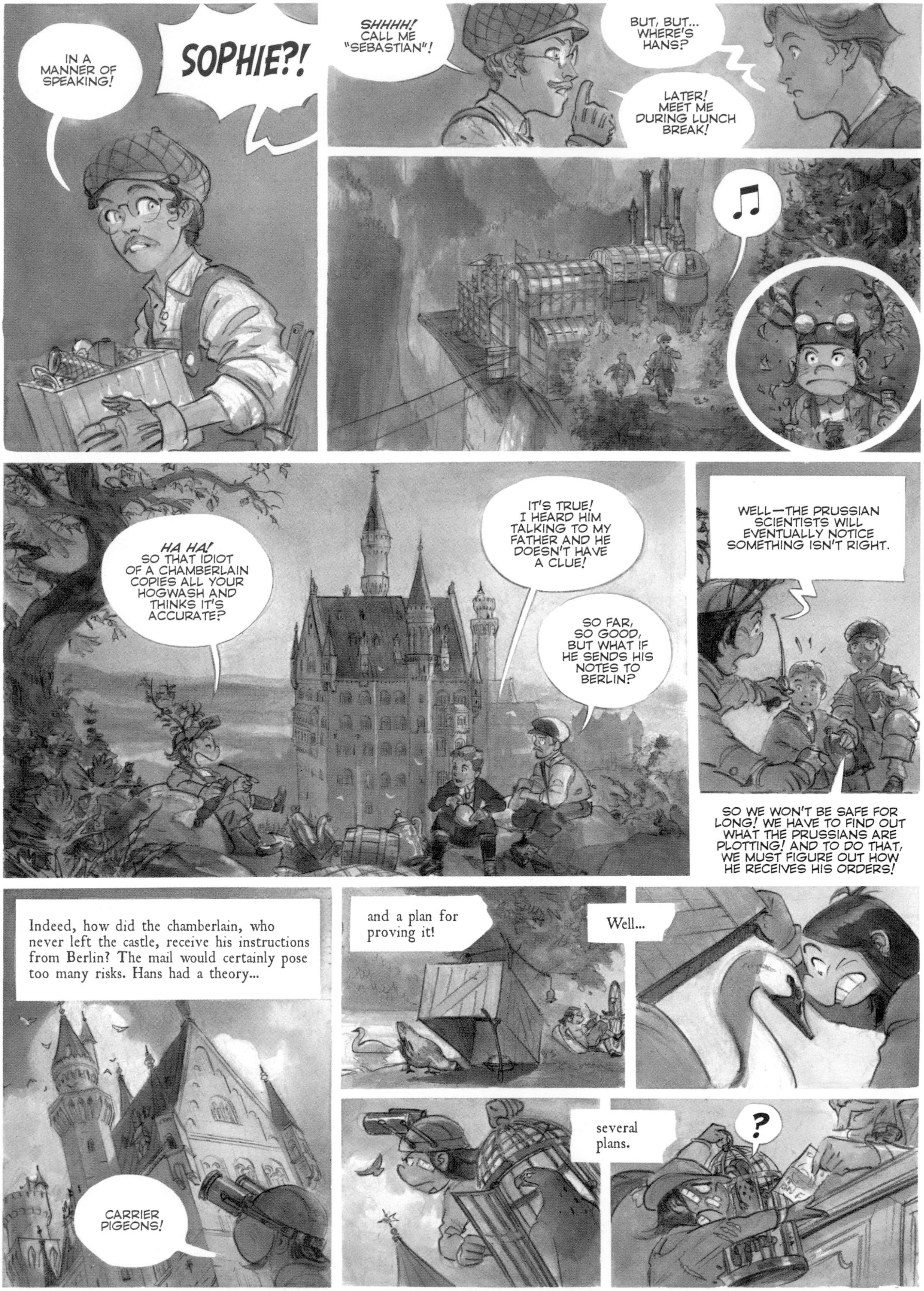
IN A MANNER OF SPEAKING!
SOPHIE?!
SHHHH! CALL ME "SEBASTIAN"!
BUT, BUT... WHERE'S HANS?
LATER! MEET ME DURING LUNCH BREAK!
♫
HA HA! SO THAT IDIOT OF A CHAMBERLAIN COPIES ALL YOUR HOGWASH AND THINKS IT'S ACCURATE?
IT'S TRUE! I HEARD HIM TALKING TO MY FATHER AND HE DOESN'T HAVE A CLUE!
SO FAR, SO GOOD, BUT WHAT IF HE SENDS HIS NOTES TO BERLIN?
WELL—THE PRUSSIAN SCIENTISTS WILL EVENTUALLY NOTICE SOMETHING ISN'T RIGHT.
SO WE WON'T BE SAFE FOR LONG! WE HAVE TO FIND OUT WHAT THE PRUSSIANS ARE PLOTTING! AND TO DO THAT, WE MUST FIGURE OUT HOW HE RECEIVES HIS ORDERS!
Indeed, how did the chamberlain, who never left the castle, receive his instructions from Berlin? The mail would certainly pose too many risks. Hans had a theory...
CARRIER PIGEONS!
and a plan for proving it!
Well...
several plans.
?

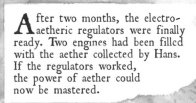

After two months, the electro-aetheric regulators were finally ready. Two engines had been filled with the aether collected by Hans. If the regulators worked, the power of aether could now be mastered.

For the occasion, the king, who never received anyone at the castle, had invited his cousin.

Needless to say, the king's cousin could not be just anyone...

But still, if a classmate had told me that one day I would be kissing the hand of the empress of Austria, I'm not sure I would have believed him.

She was the most beautiful woman I had ever seen. Since I knew no one could possibly disagree, I said as much to Sophie.

I even insisted!

But what do you expect?

!

Girls are strange.

LUDWIG, YOU KNOW YOUR PEOPLE LOVE YOU...

THEY'VE PUT UP WITH YOUR OPERAS, YOUR CASTLES... BUT NOW THIS! A FLYING MACHINE, AETHER...

IF THE PRESS SHOULD LEARN WHAT'S HAPPENING HERE...

LUDWIG, YOU AREN'T AWARE OF THE RUMORS SWIRLING ABOUT YOU...

YOU *MUST* TRAVEL TO MUNICH. YOU *MUST* ATTEND THE MINISTERS' COUNCIL...

YOUR MAJESTY... WE'RE READY!

PROCEED, PROFESSOR!

DON'T WORRY, ELISABETH. MY SUBJECTS ARE LOYAL TO ME.

SAINTS PRESERVE US!

SERAPHIN, SET THE REGULATOR FOR MINIMAL POWER AND ACTIVATE ON MY SIGNAL!

THREE,

TWO,

ONE...

ACTIVATE!

CLICK!

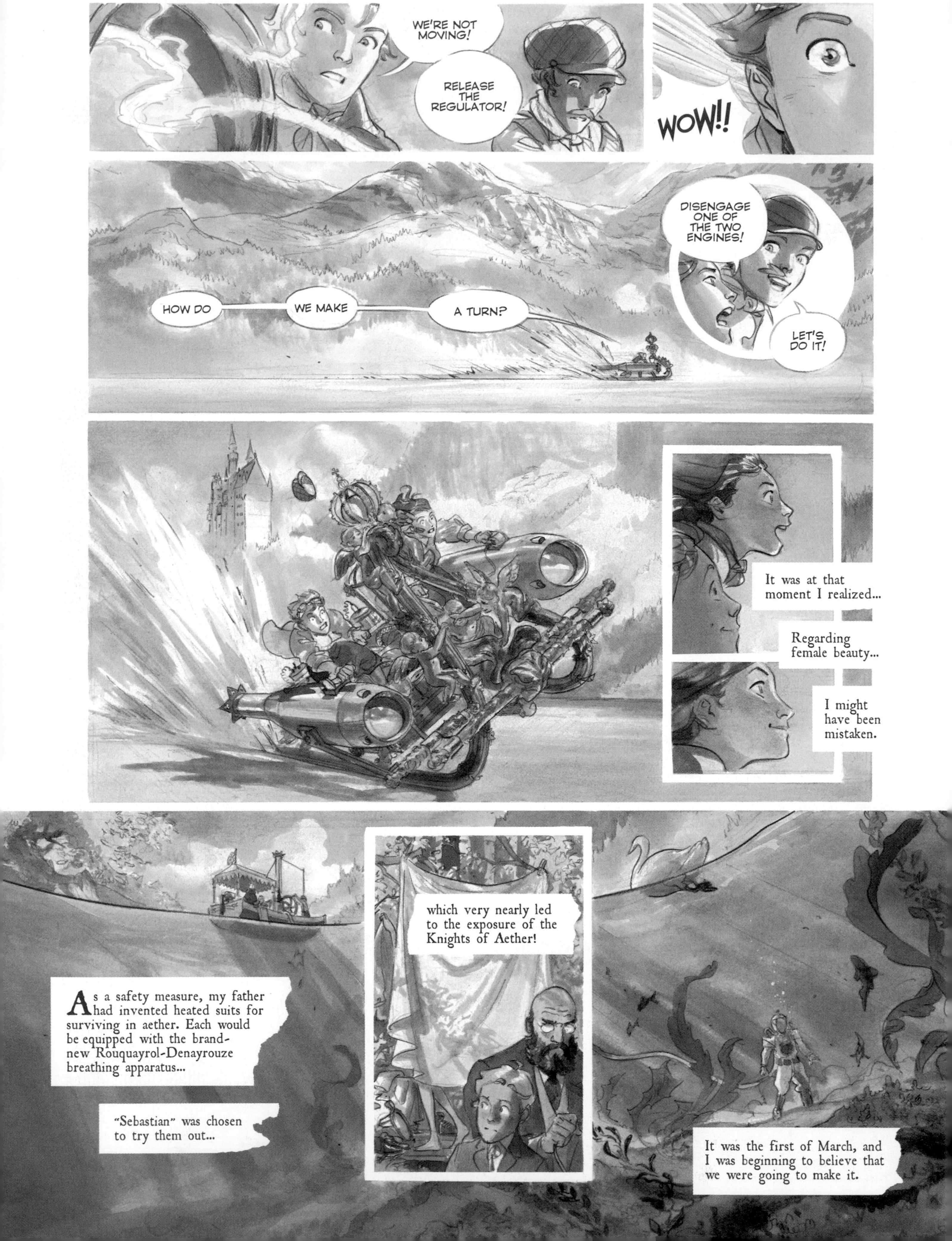
WE'RE NOT MOVING!
RELEASE THE REGULATOR!
WOW!!
HOW DO
WE MAKE
A TURN?
DISENGAGE ONE OF THE TWO ENGINES!
LET'S DO IT!
It was at that moment I realized...
Regarding female beauty...
I might have been mistaken.
As a safety measure, my father had invented heated suits for surviving in aether. Each would be equipped with the brand-new Rouquayrol-Denayrouze breathing apparatus...
"Sebastian" was chosen to try them out...
which very nearly led to the exposure of the Knights of Aether!
It was the first of March, and I was beginning to believe that we were going to make it.

Then came the day we had dreaded.

The chamberlain stopped visiting the strongbox.

The Prussians had caught on.

From now on, anything could happen...

While Bavaria was preparing to celebrate the anniversary of the king's coronation, activity at the construction site had reached a fever pitch...

We had begun the most perilous operation before the flight itself: the inflation of the balloon. To generate 100,000 cubic meters of hydrogen, a highly inflammable gas, we had to combine fifteen tons of iron filings and 8,000 liters of acid.

The evening before the launch, a ball in the king's honor was held in Munich. The whole kingdom was there, even the chamberlain. The king would then have to travel back to Swan's Rock for a launch at dawn.

No one was left at the castle except for a small garrison, my father, the king's musicians...

and us.

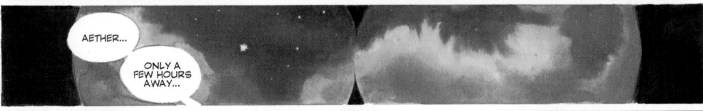

AETHER...

ONLY A FEW HOURS AWAY...

AS LONG AS YOUR FATHER DOESN'T CHANGE HIS MIND!

I'M SURE HE'LL LET ME COME ON BOARD, SOPHIE. EVERYTHING'S FUNCTIONING PROPERLY— NOTHING CAN GO WRONG!

EXCEPT SABOTAGE.

LOOK, IT'S HANS!

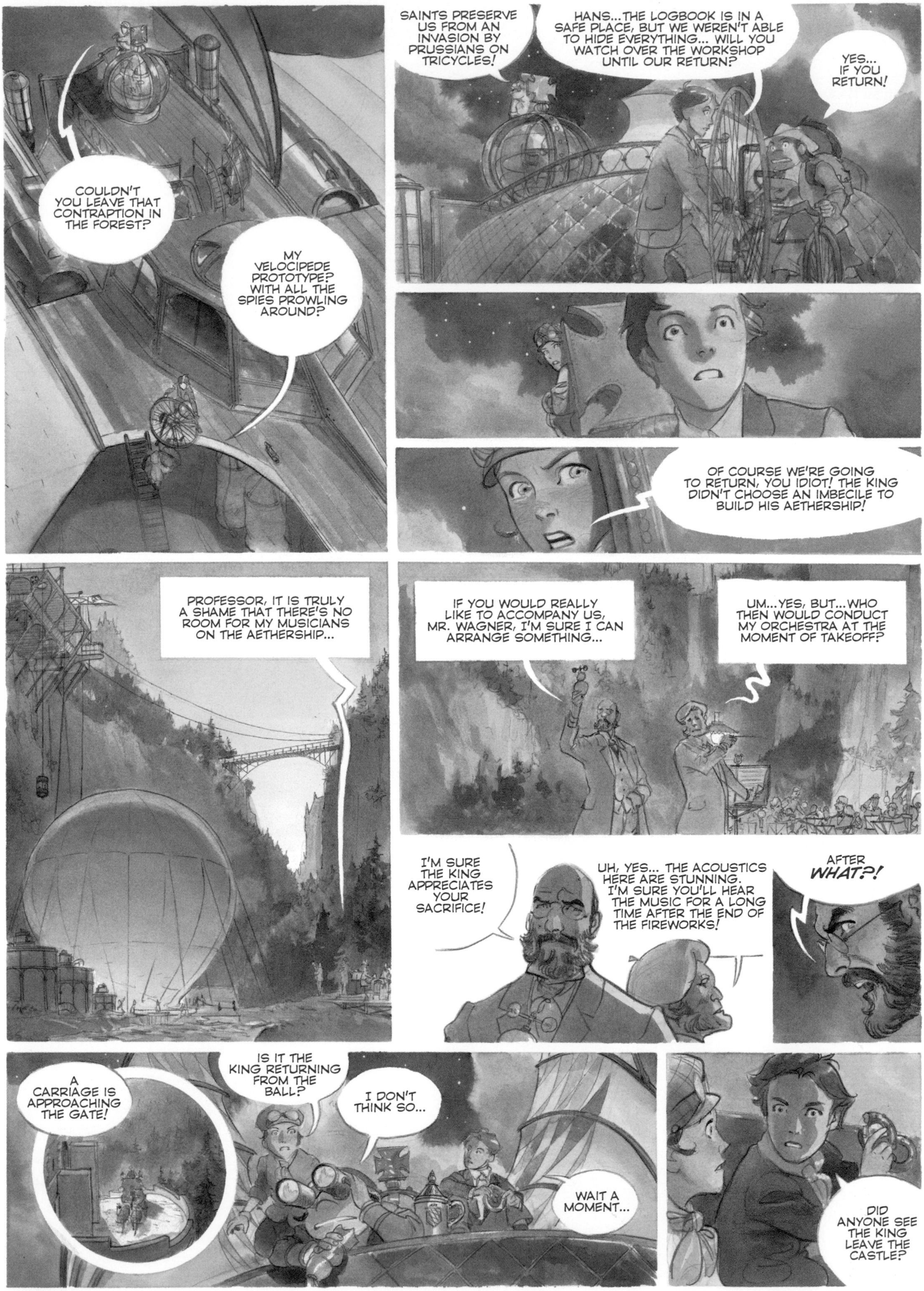
COULDN'T YOU LEAVE THAT CONTRAPTION IN THE FOREST?
MY VELOCIPEDE PROTOTYPE? WITH ALL THE SPIES PROWLING AROUND?
SAINTS PRESERVE US FROM AN INVASION BY PRUSSIANS ON TRICYCLES!
HANS...THE LOGBOOK IS IN A SAFE PLACE, BUT WE WEREN'T ABLE TO HIDE EVERYTHING... WILL YOU WATCH OVER THE WORKSHOP UNTIL OUR RETURN?
YES... IF YOU RETURN!
OF COURSE WE'RE GOING TO RETURN, YOU IDIOT! THE KING DIDN'T CHOOSE AN IMBECILE TO BUILD HIS AETHERSHIP!
PROFESSOR, IT IS TRULY A SHAME THAT THERE'S NO ROOM FOR MY MUSICIANS ON THE AETHERSHIP...
IF YOU WOULD REALLY LIKE TO ACCOMPANY US, MR. WAGNER, I'M SURE I CAN ARRANGE SOMETHING...
UM...YES, BUT...WHO THEN WOULD CONDUCT MY ORCHESTRA AT THE MOMENT OF TAKEOFF?
I'M SURE THE KING APPRECIATES YOUR SACRIFICE!
UH, YES... THE ACOUSTICS HERE ARE STUNNING. I'M SURE YOU'LL HEAR THE MUSIC FOR A LONG TIME AFTER THE END OF THE FIREWORKS!
AFTER ***WHAT?!***
A CARRIAGE IS APPROACHING THE GATE!
IS IT THE KING RETURNING FROM THE BALL?
I DON'T THINK SO...
WAIT A MOMENT...
DID ANYONE SEE THE KING LEAVE THE CASTLE?

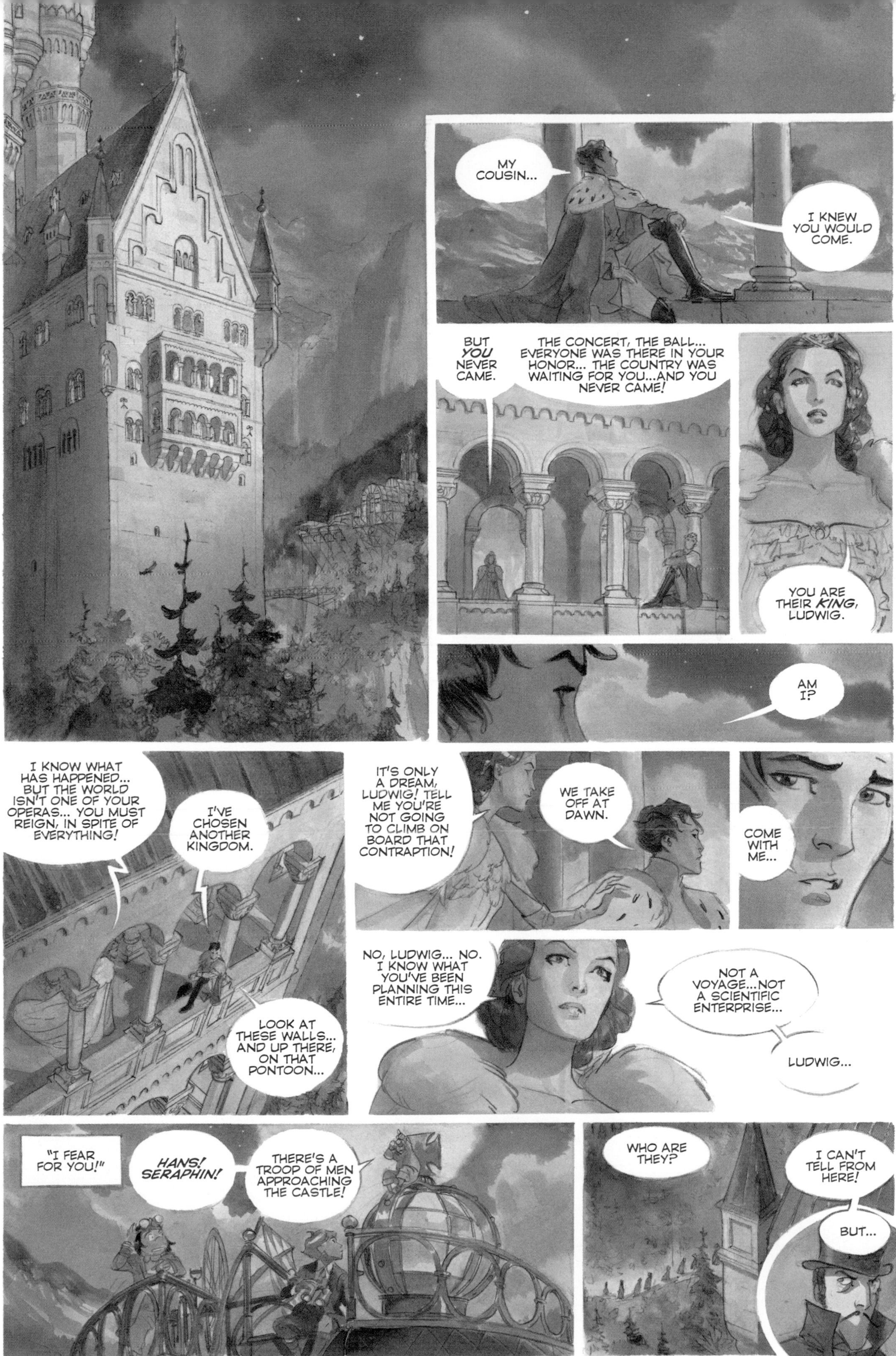
MY COUSIN...
I KNEW YOU WOULD COME.
BUT YOU NEVER CAME.
THE CONCERT, THE BALL... EVERYONE WAS THERE IN YOUR HONOR... THE COUNTRY WAS WAITING FOR YOU...AND YOU NEVER CAME!
YOU ARE THEIR KING, LUDWIG.
AM I?
I KNOW WHAT HAS HAPPENED... BUT THE WORLD ISN'T ONE OF YOUR OPERAS... YOU MUST REIGN, IN SPITE OF EVERYTHING!
I'VE CHOSEN ANOTHER KINGDOM.
LOOK AT THESE WALLS... AND UP THERE, ON THAT PONTOON...
IT'S ONLY A DREAM, LUDWIG! TELL ME YOU'RE NOT GOING TO CLIMB ON BOARD THAT CONTRAPTION!
WE TAKE OFF AT DAWN.
COME WITH ME...
NO, LUDWIG... NO. I KNOW WHAT YOU'VE BEEN PLANNING THIS ENTIRE TIME...
NOT A VOYAGE...NOT A SCIENTIFIC ENTERPRISE...
LUDWIG...
"I FEAR FOR YOU!"
HANS! SERAPHIN!
THERE'S A TROOP OF MEN APPROACHING THE CASTLE!
WHO ARE THEY?
I CAN'T TELL FROM HERE!
BUT...

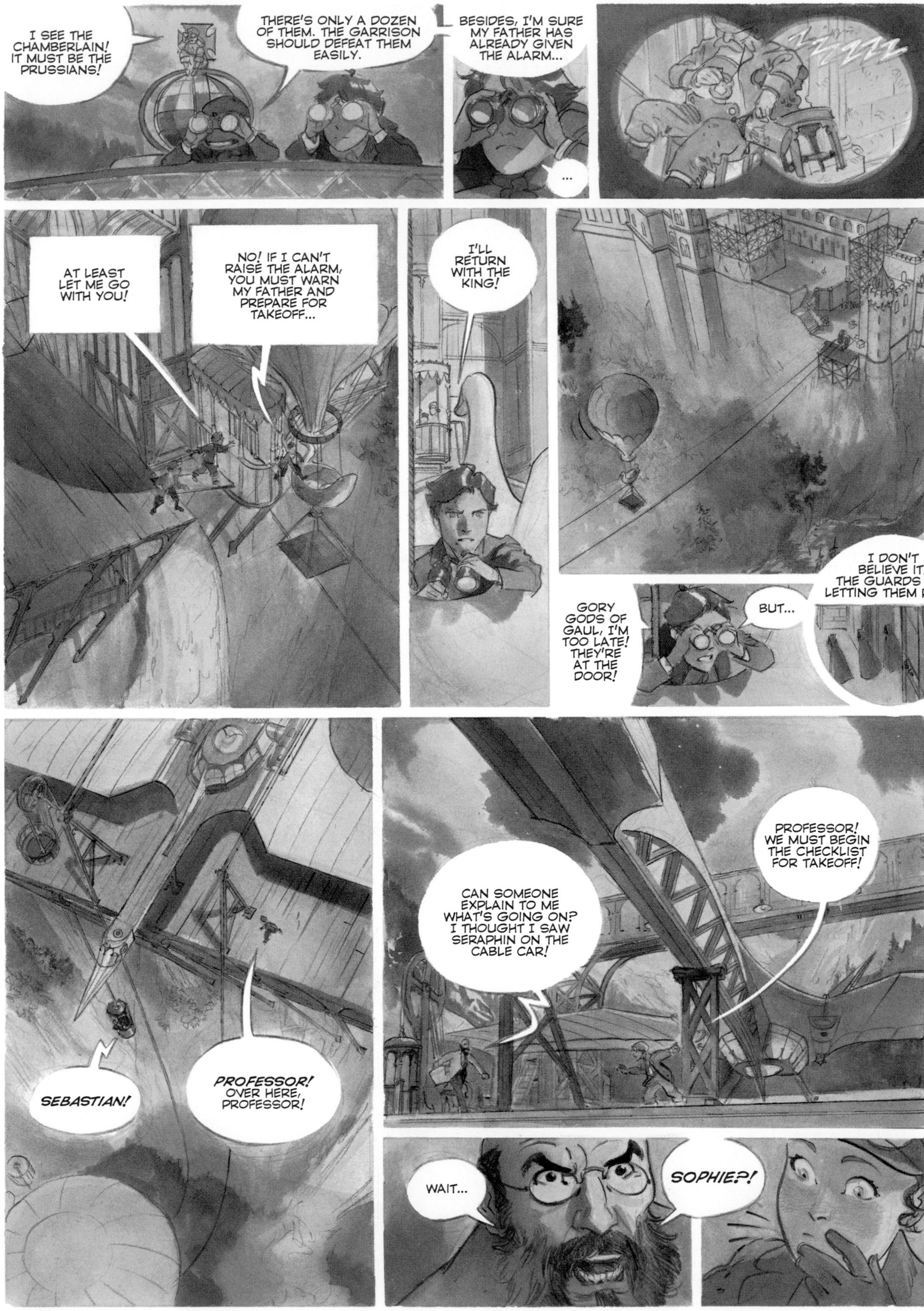

I SEE THE CHAMBERLAIN! IT MUST BE THE PRUSSIANS!
THERE'S ONLY A DOZEN OF THEM. THE GARRISON SHOULD DEFEAT THEM EASILY.
BESIDES, I'M SURE MY FATHER HAS ALREADY GIVEN THE ALARM...
...
ZZZZZZZ
AT LEAST LET ME GO WITH YOU!
NO! IF I CAN'T RAISE THE ALARM, YOU MUST WARN MY FATHER AND PREPARE FOR TAKEOFF...
I'LL RETURN WITH THE KING!
GORY GODS OF GAUL, I'M TOO LATE! THEY'RE AT THE DOOR!
BUT...
I DON'T BELIEVE IT! THE GUARDS ARE LETTING THEM PASS!
SEBASTIAN!
PROFESSOR! OVER HERE, PROFESSOR!
CAN SOMEONE EXPLAIN TO ME WHAT'S GOING ON? I THOUGHT I SAW SERAPHIN ON THE CABLE CAR!
PROFESSOR! WE MUST BEGIN THE CHECKLIST FOR TAKEOFF!
WAIT...
SOPHIE?!

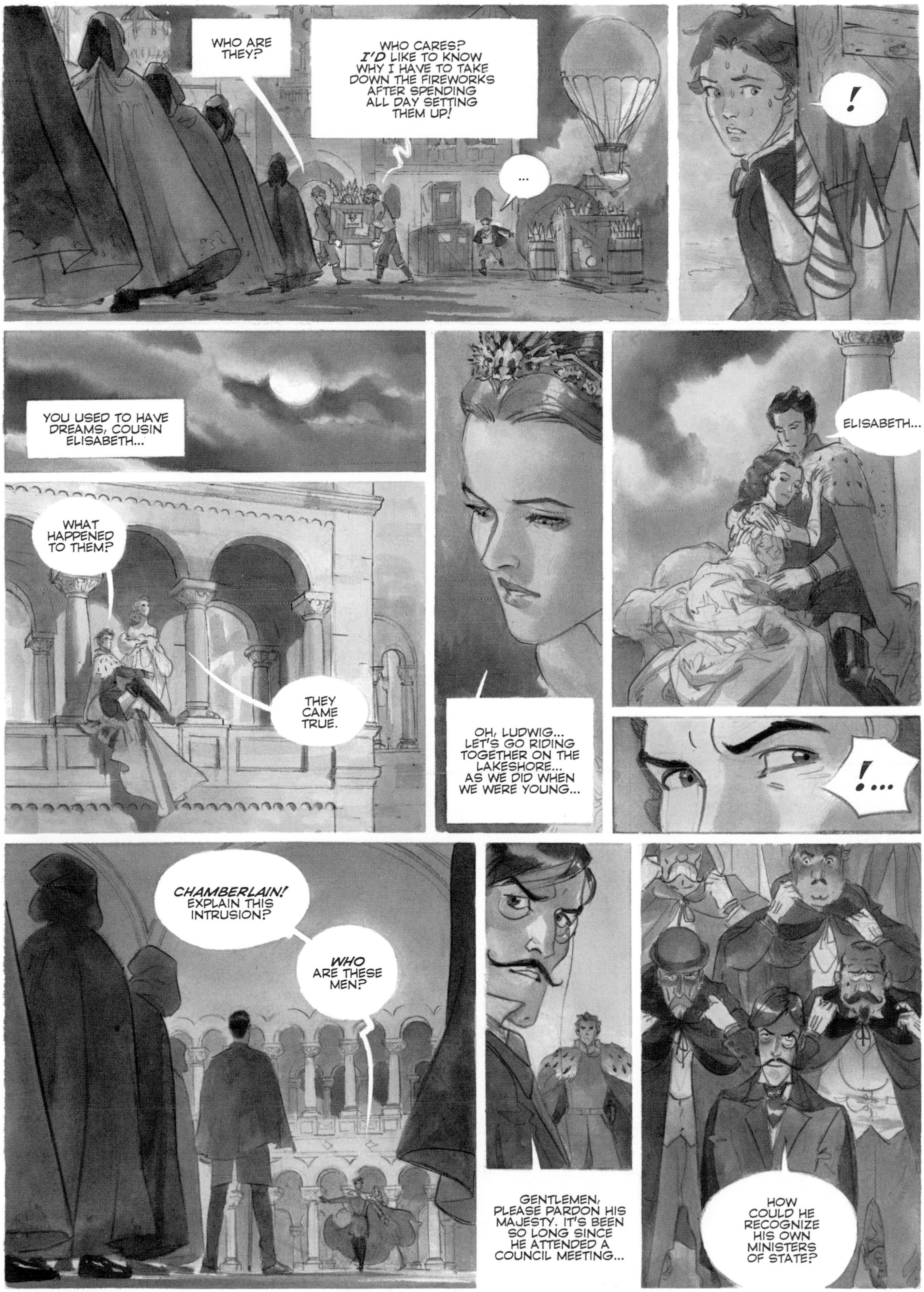
WHO ARE THEY?
WHO CARES? I'D LIKE TO KNOW WHY I HAVE TO TAKE DOWN THE FIREWORKS AFTER SPENDING ALL DAY SETTING THEM UP!
...
!
YOU USED TO HAVE DREAMS, COUSIN ELISABETH...
WHAT HAPPENED TO THEM?
THEY CAME TRUE.
OH, LUDWIG... LET'S GO RIDING TOGETHER ON THE LAKESHORE... AS WE DID WHEN WE WERE YOUNG...
ELISABETH...
!...
CHAMBERLAIN! EXPLAIN THIS INTRUSION?
WHO ARE THESE MEN?
GENTLEMEN, PLEASE PARDON HIS MAJESTY. IT'S BEEN SO LONG SINCE HE ATTENDED A COUNCIL MEETING...
HOW COULD HE RECOGNIZE HIS OWN MINISTERS OF STATE?

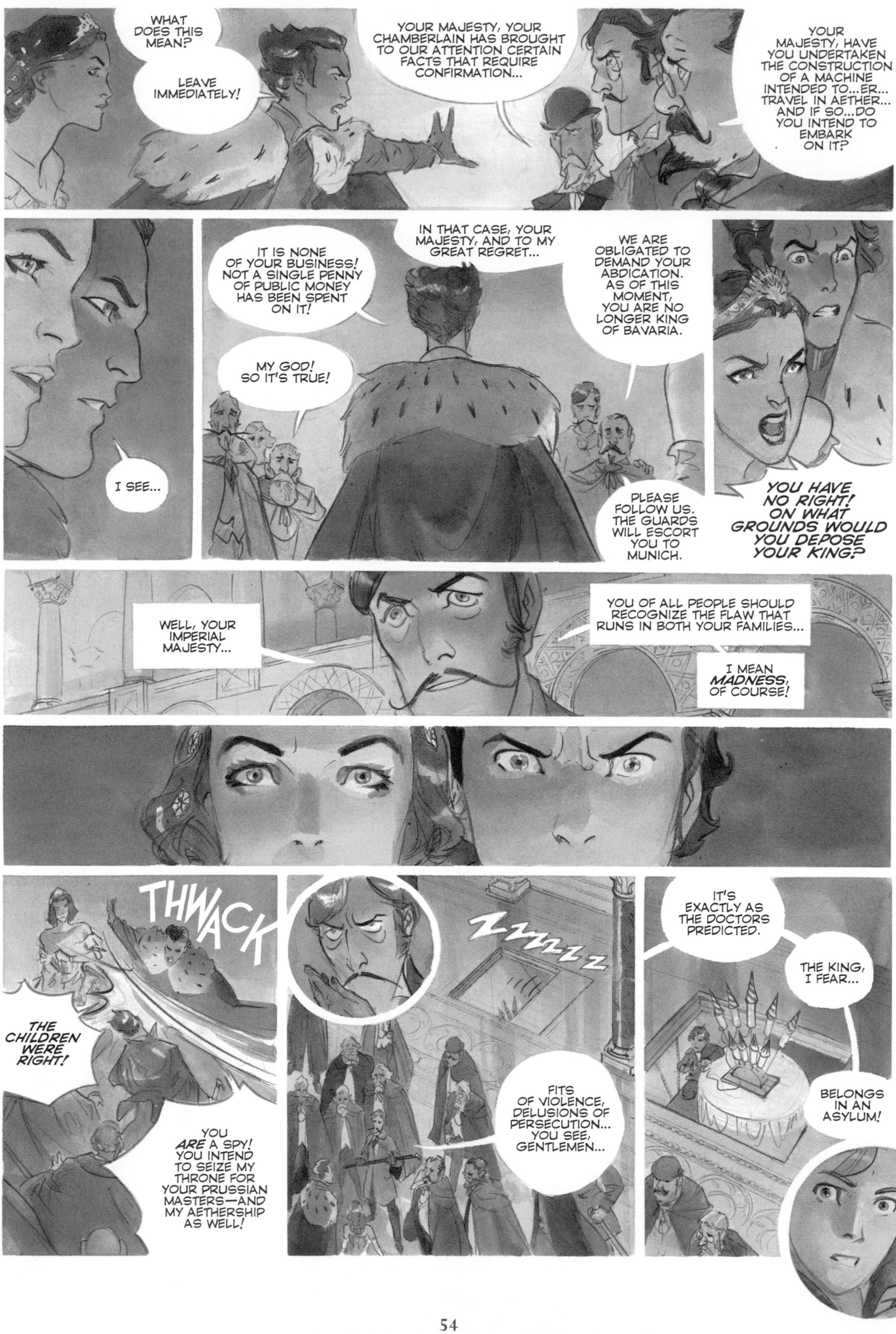

WHAT DOES THIS MEAN?
LEAVE IMMEDIATELY!
YOUR MAJESTY, YOUR CHAMBERLAIN HAS BROUGHT TO OUR ATTENTION CERTAIN FACTS THAT REQUIRE CONFIRMATION...
YOUR MAJESTY, HAVE YOU UNDERTAKEN THE CONSTRUCTION OF A MACHINE INTENDED TO...ER... TRAVEL IN AETHER... AND IF SO...DO YOU INTEND TO EMBARK ON IT?
I SEE...
IT IS NONE OF YOUR BUSINESS! NOT A SINGLE PENNY OF PUBLIC MONEY HAS BEEN SPENT ON IT!
MY GOD! SO IT'S TRUE!
IN THAT CASE, YOUR MAJESTY, AND TO MY GREAT REGRET...
WE ARE OBLIGATED TO DEMAND YOUR ABDICATION. AS OF THIS MOMENT, YOU ARE NO LONGER KING OF BAVARIA.
PLEASE FOLLOW US. THE GUARDS WILL ESCORT YOU TO MUNICH.
YOU HAVE NO RIGHT! ON WHAT GROUNDS WOULD YOU DEPOSE YOUR KING?
WELL, YOUR IMPERIAL MAJESTY...
YOU OF ALL PEOPLE SHOULD RECOGNIZE THE FLAW THAT RUNS IN BOTH YOUR FAMILIES...
I MEAN MADNESS, OF COURSE!
THWACK
THE CHILDREN WERE RIGHT!
YOU ARE A SPY! YOU INTEND TO SEIZE MY THRONE FOR YOUR PRUSSIAN MASTERS—AND MY AETHERSHIP AS WELL!
ZZZZZZZ
FITS OF VIOLENCE, DELUSIONS OF PERSECUTION... YOU SEE, GENTLEMEN...
IT'S EXACTLY AS THE DOCTORS PREDICTED.
THE KING, I FEAR...
BELONGS IN AN ASYLUM!

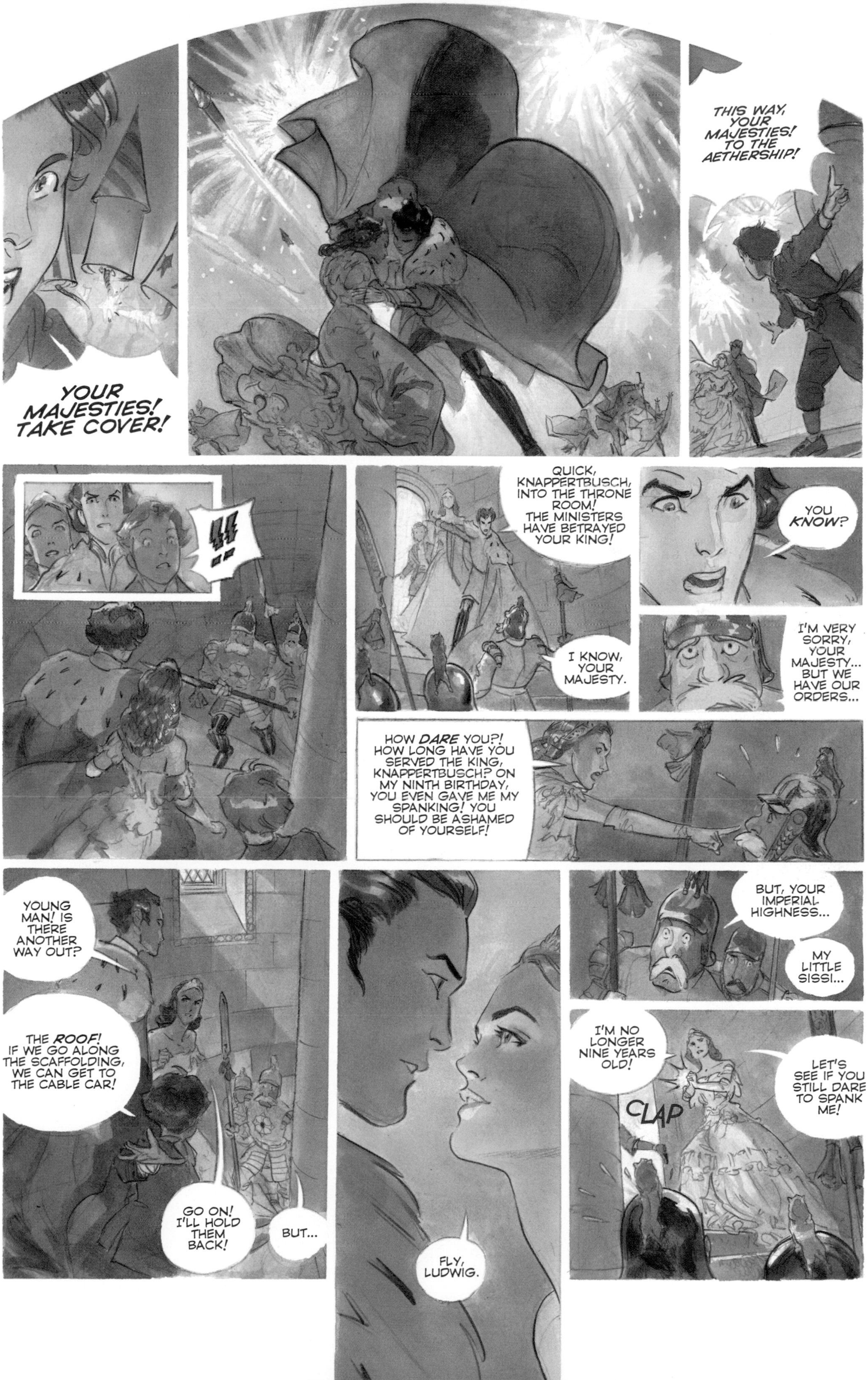
YOUR MAJESTIES! TAKE COVER!
THIS WAY, YOUR MAJESTIES! TO THE AETHERSHIP!
!!
QUICK, KNAPPERTBUSCH, INTO THE THRONE ROOM! THE MINISTERS HAVE BETRAYED YOUR KING!
I KNOW, YOUR MAJESTY.
YOU KNOW?
I'M VERY SORRY, YOUR MAJESTY... BUT WE HAVE OUR ORDERS...
HOW DARE YOU?! HOW LONG HAVE YOU SERVED THE KING, KNAPPERTBUSCH? ON MY NINTH BIRTHDAY, YOU EVEN GAVE ME MY SPANKING! YOU SHOULD BE ASHAMED OF YOURSELF!
YOUNG MAN! IS THERE ANOTHER WAY OUT?
THE ROOF! IF WE GO ALONG THE SCAFFOLDING, WE CAN GET TO THE CABLE CAR!
GO ON! I'LL HOLD THEM BACK!
BUT...
FLY, LUDWIG.
BUT, YOUR IMPERIAL HIGHNESS...
MY LITTLE SISSI...
I'M NO LONGER NINE YEARS OLD!
CLAP
LET'S SEE IF YOU STILL DARE TO SPANK ME!

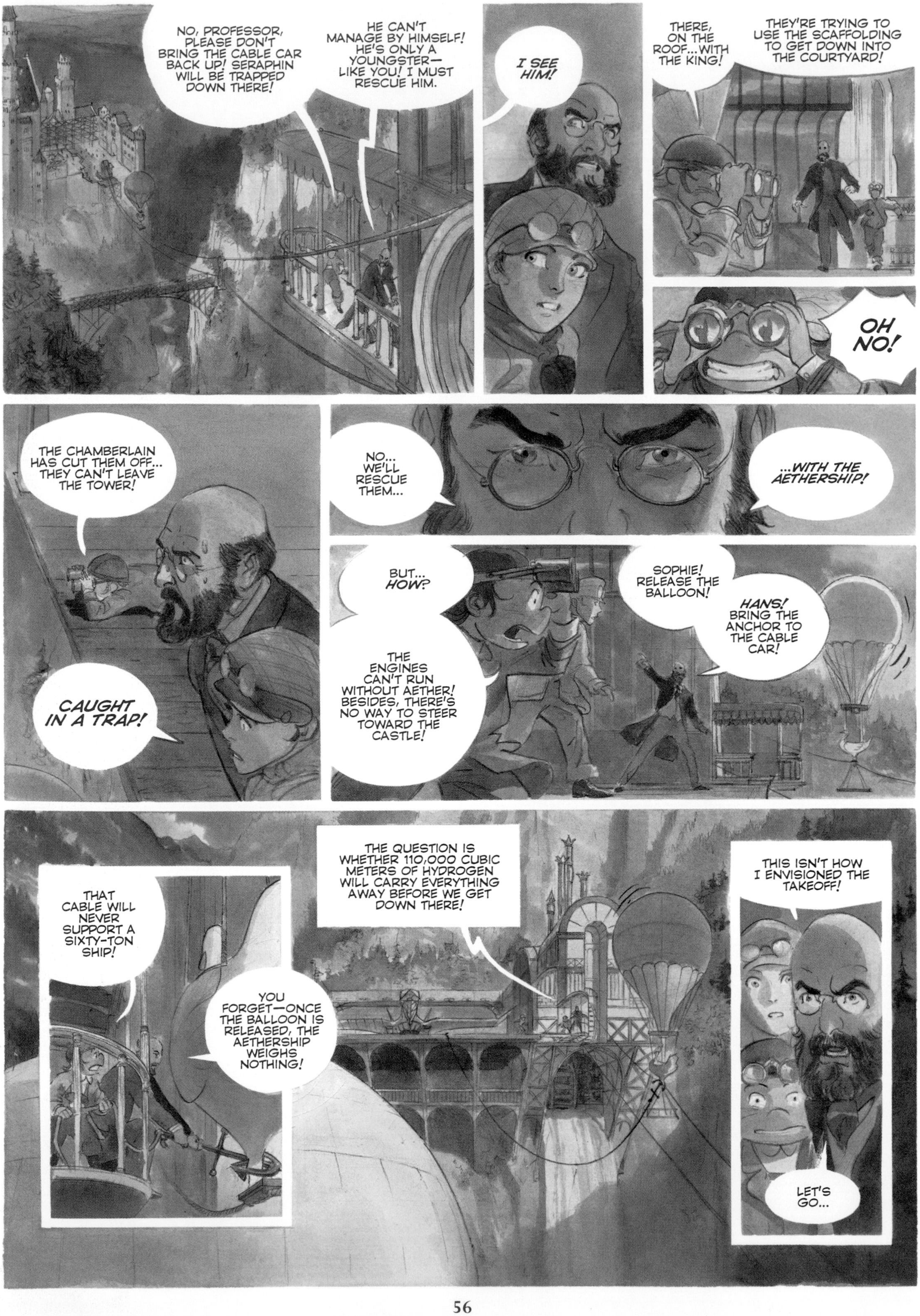
NO, PROFESSOR, PLEASE DON'T BRING THE CABLE CAR BACK UP! SERAPHIN WILL BE TRAPPED DOWN THERE!
HE CAN'T MANAGE BY HIMSELF! HE'S ONLY A YOUNGSTER— LIKE YOU! I MUST RESCUE HIM.
I SEE HIM!
THERE, ON THE ROOF...WITH THE KING!
THEY'RE TRYING TO USE THE SCAFFOLDING TO GET DOWN INTO THE COURTYARD!
OH NO!
THE CHAMBERLAIN HAS CUT THEM OFF... THEY CAN'T LEAVE THE TOWER!
CAUGHT IN A TRAP!
NO... WE'LL RESCUE THEM...
...WITH THE AETHERSHIP!
BUT... HOW?
THE ENGINES CAN'T RUN WITHOUT AETHER! BESIDES, THERE'S NO WAY TO STEER TOWARD THE CASTLE!
SOPHIE! RELEASE THE BALLOON!
HANS! BRING THE ANCHOR TO THE CABLE CAR!
THAT CABLE WILL NEVER SUPPORT A SIXTY-TON SHIP!
YOU FORGET—ONCE THE BALLOON IS RELEASED, THE AETHERSHIP WEIGHS NOTHING!
THE QUESTION IS WHETHER 110,000 CUBIC METERS OF HYDROGEN WILL CARRY EVERYTHING AWAY BEFORE WE GET DOWN THERE!
THIS ISN'T HOW I ENVISIONED THE TAKEOFF!
LET'S GO...

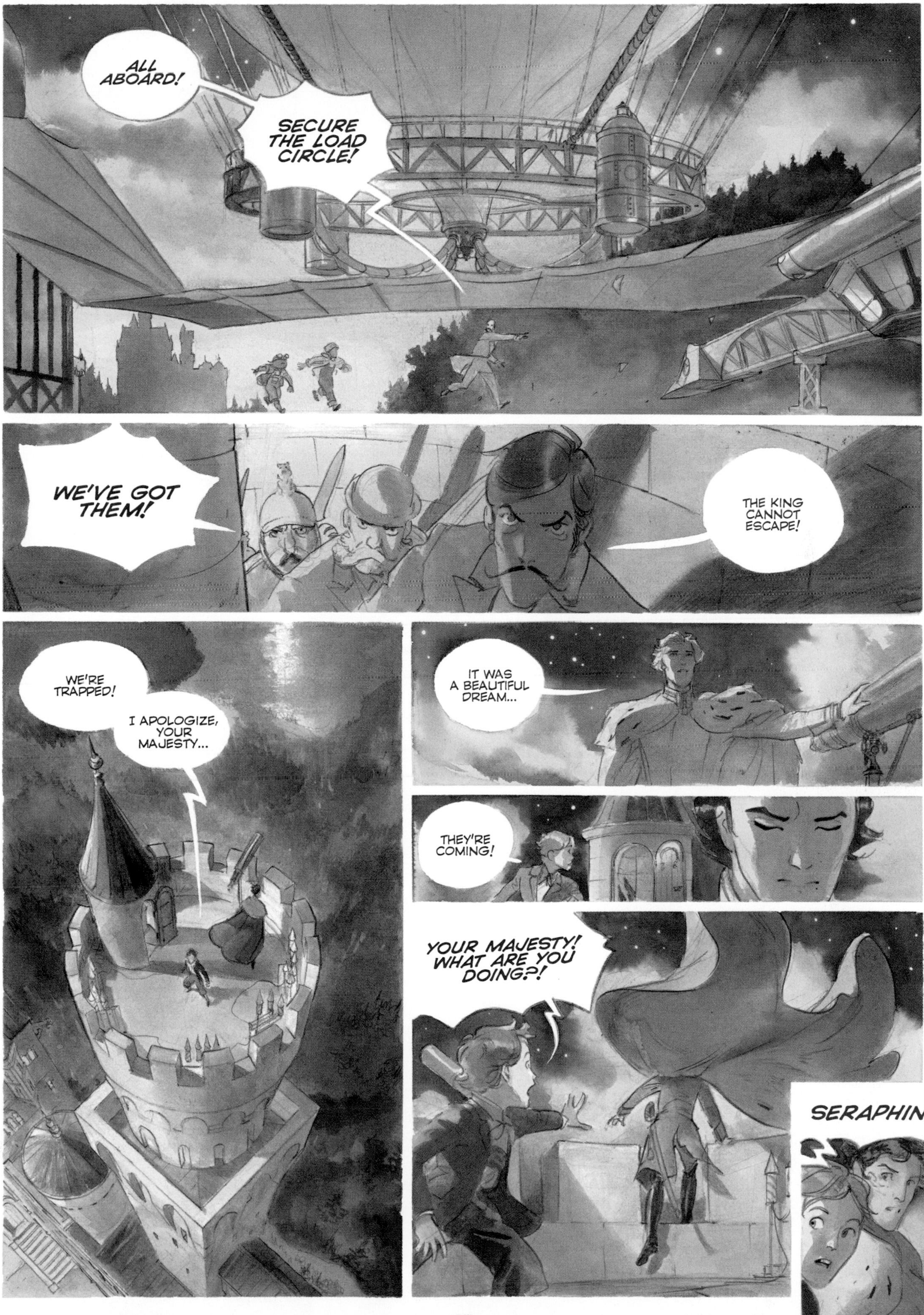
ALL ABOARD!
SECURE THE LOAD CIRCLE!
WE'VE GOT THEM!
THE KING CANNOT ESCAPE!
WE'RE TRAPPED!
I APOLOGIZE, YOUR MAJESTY...
IT WAS A BEAUTIFUL DREAM...
THEY'RE COMING!
YOUR MAJESTY! WHAT ARE YOU DOING?!
SERAPHIN!

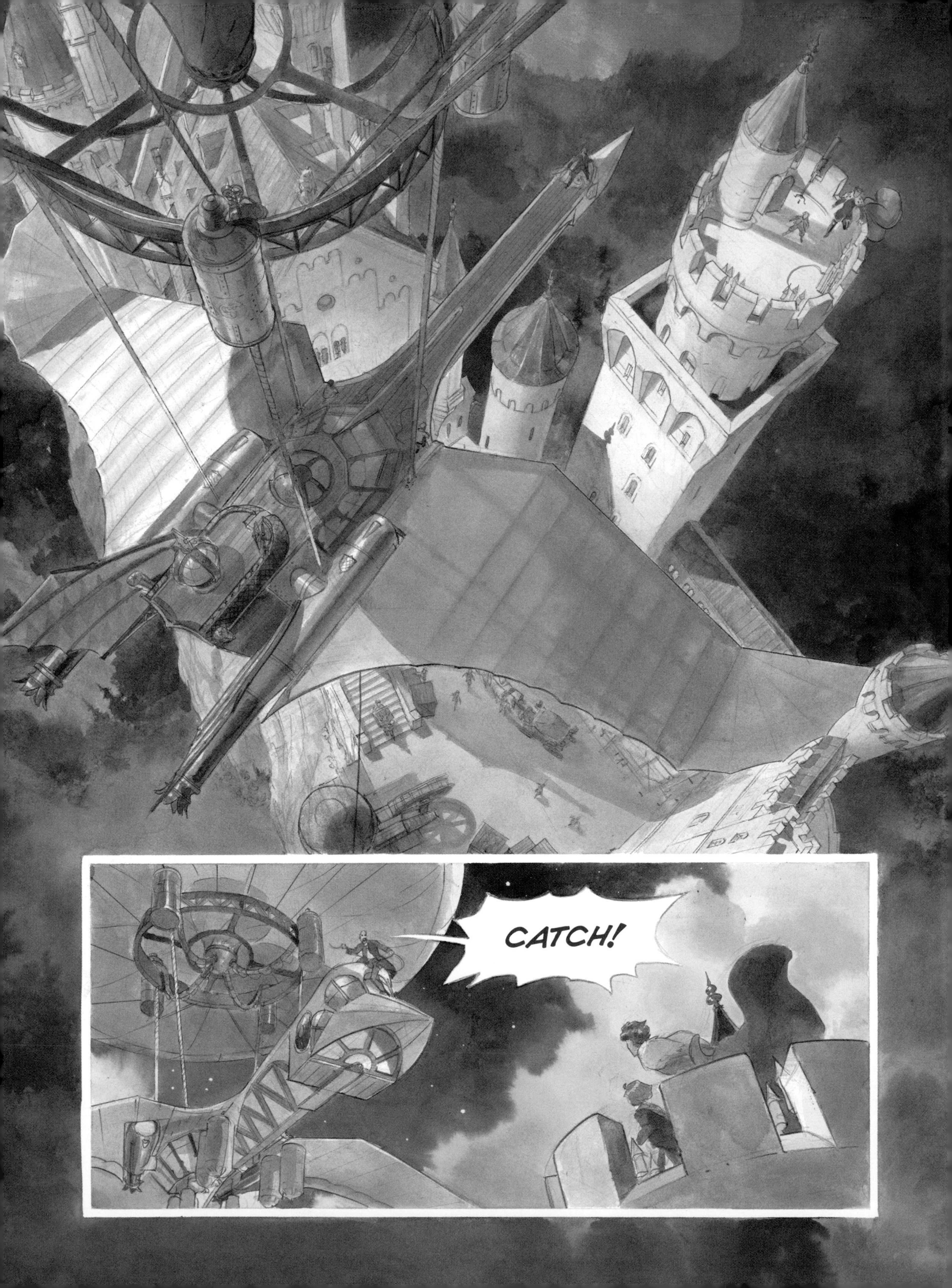
CATCH!

USE THIS TO GET US CLOSER!

GORY GODS OF GAUL, THEY'RE HERE!

HA!

HANS! SOPHIE! DROP THE BALLAST! RELEASE EVERYTHING!

AYE-AYE, SIR!

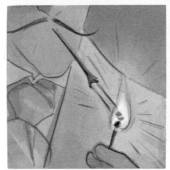

HAPPY ANNIVERSARY, YOUR MAJESTY.

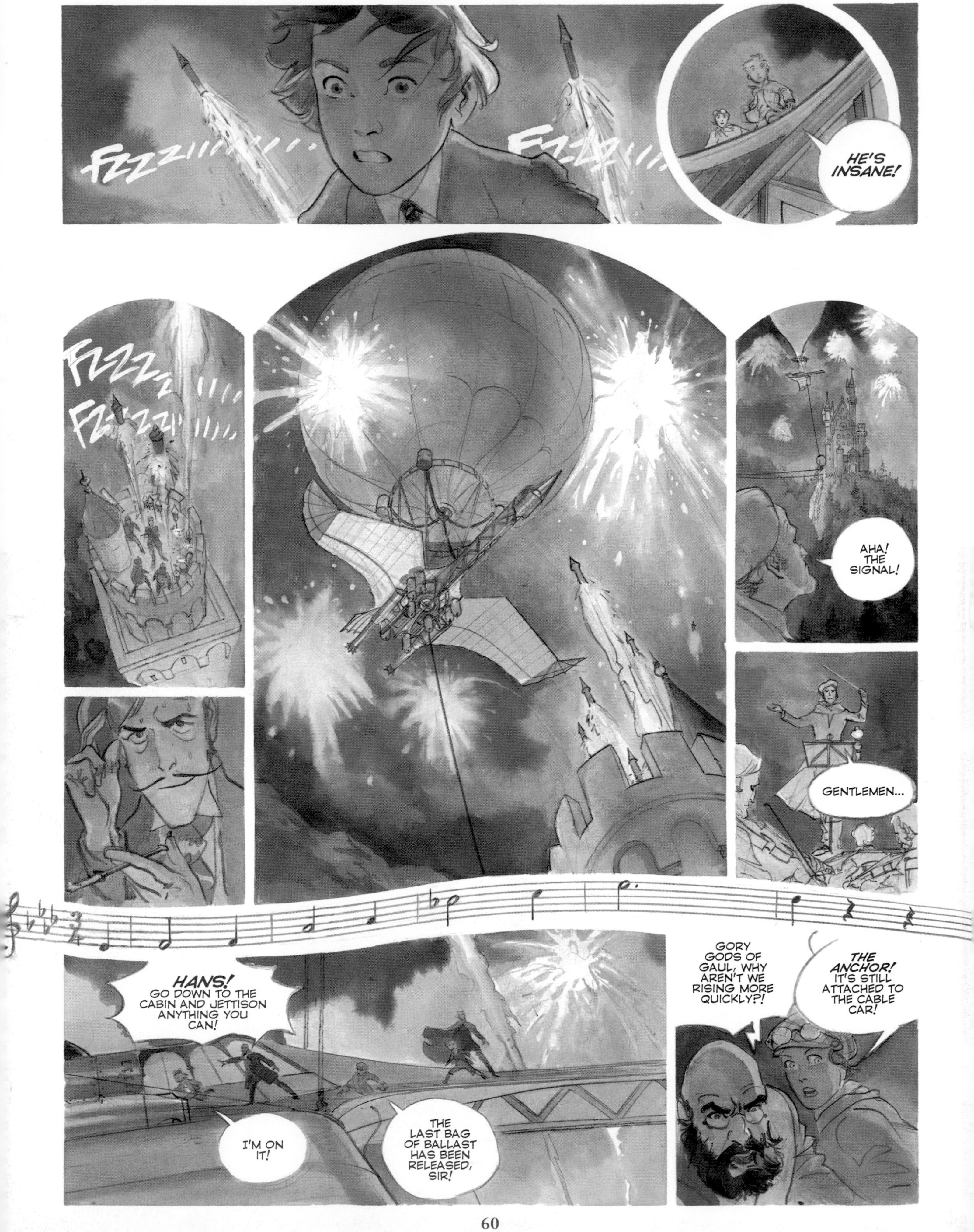
FZZZIII...
FZZZIII...
HE'S INSANE!
FZZZZ
FZZZZ...
AHA! THE SIGNAL!
GENTLEMEN...
HANS! GO DOWN TO THE CABIN AND JETTISON ANYTHING YOU CAN!
I'M ON IT!
THE LAST BAG OF BALLAST HAS BEEN RELEASED, SIR!
GORY GODS OF GAUL, WHY AREN'T WE RISING MORE QUICKLY?!
THE ANCHOR! IT'S STILL ATTACHED TO THE CABLE CAR!

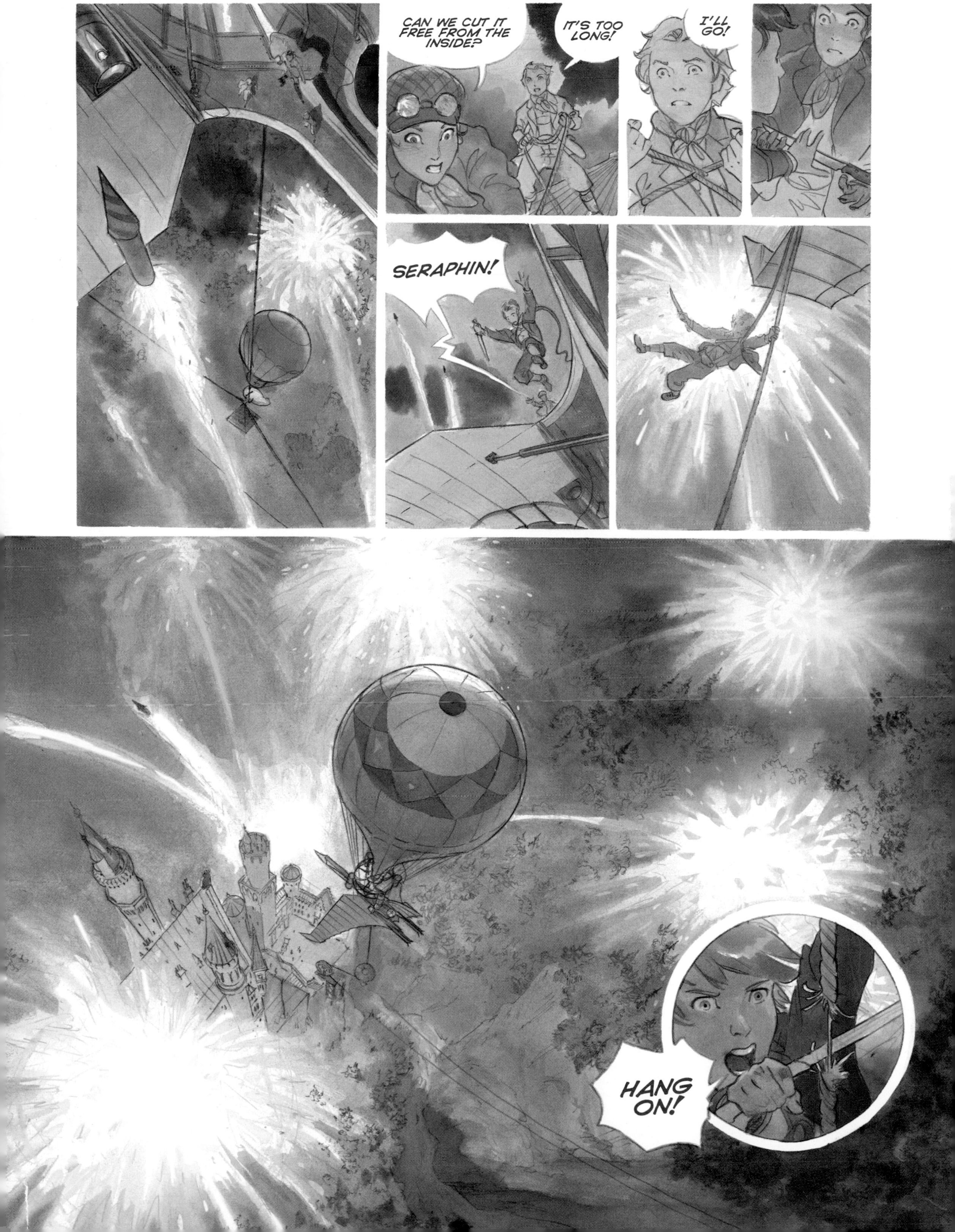
CAN WE CUT IT FREE FROM THE INSIDE?
IT'S TOO LONG!
I'LL GO!
SERAPHIN!
HANG ON!